A Bone to Pick

Stephen Oppenheimer

Praise for 'A Bone To Pick'

"Fast-paced, economical storytelling a la Ken Follett, and ironic humorous adventures, a la P.G.Wodehouse, make this an entertaining and absorbing read. England in the first half of the 20th Century, with pastoral, urban and academic scenes, along with an array of characters who span society make for a series of adventures that all have one common element-Mr. Pettibone. As he'd say, this book is 'First class. Absolutely first class.'"

-Richard B., Amazon Review

"I absolutely loved this book and devoured it in several short sittings. Excellent writing and character development. Intriguing stories. And more than a few nods to Conan Doyle's plots and pacing. Please give us more Stephen!!!"

-Gary D., Amazon Review

"Oppenheimer skilfully weaves a narrative filled with intrigue, mystery, and murder. As the story unfolds, the reader is drawn into a world where self-directed morality guides the actions of the characters. The paths they traverse are strange and uncertain, leading to unexpected twists and turns that keep the reader guessing until the very end. The author's attention to detail and historical accuracy bring the 1930s era to life, immersing the reader in a bygone time of elegance and danger. Oppenheimer's writing style is evocative, capturing the essence of the characters and their surroundings, transporting the reader to the opulent decksoftheQueenMary."

A Bone To Pick is a masterfully crafted mystery that will appeal to fans of historical fiction and detective novels. Stephen Oppenheimer proves himself to be a skilled storyteller, delivering a tale rich in atmosphere, suspense, and unexpected revelations. This book is a delightful journey into the intrigues of a bygone era, and readers will find themselves eagerly turning the pages to uncover the truth lurking beneath the surface of Mr. Pettibone's enigmatic persona."

-Emilysmom, Goodreads Review

"As a lover of British novels and TV shows this collection of interwoven stories is right up my alley. It's a very authentic and compelling journey into a long-gone time filled with interesting characters and meaningful moments large and small."

-Laura C., Amazon Review

"For people who like Agatha Christie detective-style novels it will be a real gift and joy to read "A Bone To Pick: The Adventures of Mr.Pettibone Among Others". This book represents and nicely shows a very interesting combination of human nature in all of it manifestations."

-Alex., Amazon Review

"...a wonderful collection of stories chronicling the lives and adventures of a group of strangers traveling the world and discovering truths about each other along the way. Each story is delightful on its own, but the real joy is seeing how Oppenheimer weaves each thread together into a beautiful tapestry."

-Gadget., Amazon Review

BOOKS BY STEPHEN OPPENHEIMER

In Preparation
Featuring Mr. Pettibone:

Reflections' Glass
Worse Confounded
Crosstalk

Other:
The Devil Lies in the Past

ISBN 9798988214205

This is a work of fiction.
Any resemblance to any person living or dead is unintentional and accidental.

Website:stephenoppenheimer.com

For Susan- in recognition of a debt that I can never repay.

Part 1: All at Sea

Chapter 1: Absolutely First Class

Springing with a much lighter step from the railway carriage than would be expected of someone so portly, Mr. Pettibone stopped and rubbed his hands together. The glee shone through, and a sudden glint of sunlight embraced the gentle brown eyes and embellished his cherubic countenance. Here he was at last. Ever since the reports of the maiden voyage of the Queen Mary in 1936, he wanted so desperately to book a passage. A widower of several years, he had saved up enough for this special occasion and so, throwing caution to the winds, he booked not a suite — that would be beyond him — but a fine outside double, for single occupancy. First class. As the well-dressed passed him by en route to the Ocean Terminal passenger embarkation lines, he was aware of his off-the-peg gray suit, and subconsciously picked at the waistcoat, smoothing out imaginary creases.

And he was truly rubbing shoulders with the upper crust. If asked about his employment, Mr. Pettibone would reply that he was a sort of accountant; but no, there were no letters after his name. His parents were too poor for any education further than the Board Schools permitted to 14 years of age. In his very carriage on the way down from London, in the seat directly across had sat a very distinguished-looking man, probably in his forties, just like Mr. Pettibone. Despite being from different backgrounds, they started to chat and found common interests: cricket, the turf (Mr. Pettibone liked a flutter), cards, and ballet. No, they had not been at Dorchester School together, nor at Cardinal

College, Oxford. Fancy that toff thinking that someone like him would have been to any such posh places, or even have heard of them. He was a real gent, and on giving Mr. Pettibone his card, had said:

"When you get settled old man, we'll have a drink together and spin a few yarns. I'd say you have much to talk about. You seem to be a man of the world."

Mr. Pettibone involuntarily patted the coat breast pocket in which he had delicately placed the toff's card. Major Sir John Cylburn-Buller, Bt, DSO, MC it had said, late of the Staybrookshire Regiment. Absolutely first class. Who would have thought that old Petti would be rubbing shoulders with aristos? And he picked up his valise and ran after the porter who was rapidly wheeling his luggage towards the terminal.

Only a glimpse of the immense size of the liner was visible as he ran up the gangplank (first-class passengers only) and was received by the purser as he reached the ship's entry. A page took his valise, and in a cockney accent much more marked than that of Mr. Pettibone, led him to his cabin. A vague feeling of disappointment swept over Mr. Pettibone as he entered; no flowers, no champagne. And fluorescent lighting — the very newest thing — cast a cold glow on the walnut panelling. But he soon cheered up and giving the page a wink and a half-crown ("Cor!" said the page) recovered his customary good humour.

Dinner that evening was an informal one, thank goodness, for Mr. Pettibone felt uncomfortable in evening clothes. To his delight, he discovered he was seated next to Sir John at a table hosted by the second engineer. Across from him were a pleasant American couple, a banker and his wife, Mr. and Mrs. Clearwater. A rather sour German couple, the Baron and Baroness von Fresheim, made up the remainder. Mr. Pettibone was rather overawed and sat silently for a while, his eyes wandering over the guests and absorbing the gentle hum of conversation and the soft murmur of the engines. A feeling of general well-being spread over him. Smiling benignly, he admired the splendid jewelry the ladies wore, although he would be the first to admit that he could not distinguish diamonds from paste.

Sir John's words suddenly caught his attention, and he realized that he was being asked a question.

"What about a quick game of bridge before bed? And you, Baron and Mrs. Baron? Care to join us?"

"Capital," he said after some discussion and not taking no for an answer.

At the table that the Major had the foresight to reserve in advance, a lavish sequence of malts was served, with brandy (not cognac) for the Americans. Everyone was merry and became more so as the evening wore on. The Germans decided to observe and were settled on a settee not far from the table, drinking Sekt and making comments in their language. Mr. Pettibone was sure that they were laughing at him. So what? he thought. I've paid for my ticket and have every right to be here, even if I'm not rich or a toff; and he underlined that thought with a barely stifled hiccough. After a while, the Baron got up and left the room.

"Not really much of a hand at bridge," said Mr. Pettibone. "Poker's more my line."

But surprisingly, Mr. Pettibone won each rubber and collected a rather large amount of cash.

"Gosh," he said as he took out his wallet to stow his winnings.

"Looks like you're already stacked," said the Major, glancing at the thick wad of notes it barely contained.

"Always have cash on you. Even if it's less than a quid," Mr. Pettibone replied. "Never know when you might need it; that's what my old dad used to say. Anyway, it's rather late and I need my shuteye." He beamed at the group. "Nighty-night all, and see you tomorrow." And off he went to bed with a light step.

Mr. Pettibone awoke in the morning with a slight hangover, then counted his winnings. "About 250 pounds," he said aloud. "Christ!" And he shook his head barely believing his good fortune. He carefully separated the notes comprising his winnings and put them in an envelope to be placed in the purser's safe. The other notes, his own, he kept in his wallet, to which he added more after taking them from his valise.

Just before lunch, a glass of stout in his hand, Mr. Pettibone noticed the rich Americans on their own in a secluded part of the Verandah Bar. He walked up to them from behind, swaying just as the boat made a slight lurch. Recovering his balance, he brushed against Mrs. Clearwater.

"I'm ever so sorry, madame," he said, "not too steady this AM. Too much to drink yesterday."

Mrs. Clearwater frowned at the glass of stout.

"Oh, that's the hair of the dog."

Mrs. Clearwater was not amused, and very shortly she and her husband got up to leave. As they did so, the Major arrived at the bar, collided with them, and spilled his drink over Mrs. Clearwater's dress. Coloring rapidly, he apologized profusely.

"Haven't quite got my sea legs yet, I'm afraid Mrs. C.," he said.

"Yes," she replied. "Mr. Pettibone was saying the same thing." And she fixed the Major with an unfriendly look.

"I say, old man. I've put together a little group of people, special ones you'll like and they would all like to meet you. I thought a little game of poker might break the ice?" The Major said this in such a charming manner that Mr. Pettibone was captivated. Playing cards with the nobs, absolutely first class, he thought. He looked up above the chair and with a short laugh pointed out the sign to the Major.

"The Management of the Cunard Line respectfully wishes to inform its passengers that they should exercise caution when playing cards with individuals not personally known to them. Cardsharps frequently travel on ocean liners."

The Major shrugged his shoulders. "I could tell you a thing or two about that," he said, "but it's time for my lunch."

All six table companions were present at lunch and the conversation turned to banking, and then money, and then the quality of banknotes.

"Now, take your five-pound note," said Mr. Clearwater. "I consider myself somewhat of an expert, collecting coins and early currency.

"He has one of the largest collections in the country," his wife chipped in. "We're going to leave it to the Smithsonian."

"Well," continued the banker, "that note of yours seems to be printed on secondhand paper and is so very easy to forge. Just look at this," and he took a note out of his pocket and unfolded it for the table to see his point. And indeed, it did look very bland. Just plain white paper with a few thick marks to establish value, a number and a signature.

"Oh, you think so, do you?" said Mr. Pettibone. "Let's see. Oh, yes." And he beamed his cherubic smile at the table. "In my line of business ..."

"Which is?" asked Mrs. Clearwater acidly.

Mr. Pettibone went on, "I have to handle large amounts of cash for clients. I'm a sort of accountant you see, Madame," he bowed slightly "and I have the privilege of handling the monetary affairs of some very rich people. Now, this note, it's so beautiful in its simplicity. Yet damned difficult — excuse the cuss words, ladies — to forge. Not only is each serial number registered with the Bank of England, but every year the Bank changes some very minute detail. For example, look at these round marks around this figure of Britannia. This is a current note, dated 1937, and I can tell you it's absolutely genuine because the sixth ball from the right is only a half-circle. Other years it was full, and there are many other similar changes I could tell you about. I have to be on my toes, you see. Wouldn't do for my clients to be foisted with imitation notes, now would it?"

Mr. Clearwater exclaimed, "Well, I'm damned."

Mr. Pettibone looked pleased with himself. He knew something these rich, well-educated people didn't.

That afternoon at about 4 p.m., he joined the card table in the Major's suite. A wonderful setting, he thought. This one had the flowers and champagne (it's alright for some, he thought) as well as some small sandwiches that a server in a short white coat and gloves handed around.

"Pettibone, this is Colonel Bailey, my old commanding officer during the war, his brother-in-law Lord Staybrook and Staybrook's son, the Hon Piers Roxbury.

"Charmed," said Mr. Pettibone and sat down at the table.

"Give Mr. Pettibone a Partagas," said the Major, and the server came round with a Dunhill humidor and opened it in front of him. "Crikey. Haven't seen cigars this big for years," said Mr. Pettibone, and he took two. Lord Staybrook looked at him strangely, and by way of explanation, Mr. Pettibone said, "One for now, my Lord, and one for later," and he gave the company such a roguish smile that they all burst out laughing.

"Oh, by the way, Pettibone, you're not a servant. So don't call him my Lord," said Sir John.

"Well, what ...?"

"Just Lord Staybrook will do. And when you get to know him, say after 10 years, you can call him Staybrook."

The game went quite well. At least at first. Mr. Pettibone won about 300 pounds, which he picked up and put in his pocket. But then his luck turned and suddenly he was down 2,000. Embarrassed and somewhat annoyed with himself, he got up.

"Gents, I think I'd better go. I can't afford to lose that much."

"Sit down, Pettibone," said Lord Staybrook. "Just a little losing streak. We all have them. Another round and then we'll let you go."

And Pettibone, delighted to be called by his name by a Peer of the Realm sat and won back 500.

"And now I really must go," he said. "Got to dress for dinner." Reckoning his losses, he glared at the group and left.

Later, as Pettibone was leaving his cabin, his steward asked whether he might have seen Mrs. Clearwater's necklace. Somewhat nonplussed, he said that he hadn't a clue. Apparently, she had lost it somewhere on the ship the steward said, and was raising all hell and making accusations left, right and centre.

"So would I if I was in her shoes," said Mr. Pettibone. "Valuable was it?"

"More sentimental value, but still worth a tidy sum," was the reply.

Mr. Pettibone shrugged his shoulders, walked into the dining room and found that he was one of only two or three in white tie. The men nearly uniformly were wearing dinner jackets. He flushed a little at this and awkwardly trod his way to the table.

"Dressed to the nines tonight, Pettibone? What's the occasion?" the Major asked.

Somewhat annoyed at the jest, Mr. Pettibone replied with uncharacteristic sharpness. "The occasion, Major, is losing 1,500 quid to you and your friends."

"I really am so sorry about that, old man. But it's a game of chance. Some skill, some strategy, a bit of acting, but mainly luck, my boy. Mainly luck. Tell you what, if you're really hard up I can lend you some cash."

Mr. Pettibone thought for a moment and said, "Tell you what, Major. I need some dollars. Could we fix an exchange rate and I'll trade with you?"

"Certainly. How much?"

"Say 5,000 pounds, that's $25,000. Could you manage that?"

"No. But I could do 2,000, which would be 10. However, there is one stipulation."

"Yes?"

"Will you come back and play cards tonight? Lord Staybrook really enjoyed your company, and his son is off chasing a rich widow. So, there will only be him, you, and me. He really is a jolly good sort, and he specifically asked for you."

Mr. Pettibone beamed, "Absolutely first class!" he said.

And play he did, initially losing and then winning, then losing again.

He got up from the table at 1 a.m. and wiped his perspiring forehead.

"You lot are too good for me, you really are." He ruefully totted up the amount. I've lost another 3,000 pounds. And that excludes the $1,000 that I won. So, I'm down 5,000 quid to you gents. Sorry but that's my lot. Oh, and by the way Major, about our transaction, I am sorry but I don't have the cash left. No more cards for me, thanks all the same. Lord Staybrook, Major, I'd like to say it's been a pleasure..."

And he left. He had hoped so much for an uncomplicated trip, and he could almost kick himself that he allowed this to happen.

Reaching the cabin, he took the 1,000 pounds that he just won, put it in an envelope, sealed it, and next day gave it to the purser.

In the bar, a flushed Mrs. Clearwater came up to him.

"Have you seen my necklace?"

"Still can't find it? I'm very sorry, Madame. Can I help you in any way? Perhaps we can reconstruct where you were about the time that you lost it?"

"Lost it? I didn't lose it, you funny little man! It was stolen."

Mr. Pettibone's good humour was sorely tried, but he was accustomed to keeping his temper.

"I don't know what to say. I doubt that anyone had the opportunity to steal it. Who would do such a thing?" And he looked around at the other passengers, all well-groomed and clearly so much at ease with life as the rich lived it."

"I don't think anyone here would need the money. Now who on earth would you think would do something like that?"

"I don't think. I know! I only ask whether people have seen the thing so that I can gauge their reaction. I'm a very good judge of character."

Mr. Pettibone looked at her askance.

"It's definitely that Sir John what's-his-name. If ever there was a fraud, it's him. As for being at Dorchester School, our son spent a year there and I wired him to find out from the headmaster if there was ever such a person in any of the houses. And you know what, they've never heard of him. But he is in Debrett."

"In … what?"

"Oh, that fat, silly red book you Englishers never travel without. A compendium of the rich, lame, and lazy. If you have a title, you're in, and he's in. No education, no clubs listed and yes, he was in the Army during the war, as a captain. No DSO and no MC."

Mr. Pettibone stared at her. "Well, I'm damned," he said.

"I think that man is a professional crook, and trades on his supposed background. Same for that Lord Straycrook or whatever. Another one. I've told the captain, and he has requested the master-at-arms to keep an eye on those two. And by the way, don't play cards with them. My husband lost a fortune yesterday, and we are not speaking."

"I hope you're wrong," said Mr. Pettibone, and walked off.

That night the ship listed severely and was caught in a typical Atlantic squall. Few people attended breakfast. Mr. Pettibone walked steadily to the first officer's office. He thought that the passengers needed cheering up, as the few he saw were green in colour and rather frightened. Particularly the children would need some fun, at least those not lying in their cabins puking their little guts out. Fortunately for him, he didn't suffer from mal de mer.

9

The first officer was friendly enough and thought his idea a good one. Mr. Pettibone's hobby was prestidigitation, not conjuring you understand. Why that was like calling the Queen Mary a boat. It's a ship of course, and just as surely a prestidigitator is not a conjuror. A conjuror saws people in half, pulls rabbits out of hats, that sort of thing. No, Mr. Pettibone absolutely insists that his audience knows that everything he does is a trick and can be easily discovered, if you just paid attention and knew what to look for. In fact, Mr. Pettibone challenges the audience to discover his ploys and actually will show them how one or two are done. So, if the first officer would make an announcement … And the first officer did.

The show went well. There was a limited audience as the sea was still rough, with about five children of whom in one way or another he made use during his tricks. No one was able to see how he cast his illusions.

"So, you see, ladies and gents, that when I show you how it was done, you'll all say, "Of course; it's really simple."

And he showed them, and they all said how simple it was. Chuckling with good humour, Mr. Pettibone left the room to gales of laughter and applause. "Absolutely first class," he said to himself:
'Well, Pettibone old man, you're not so unpopular after all.'

The day of disembarkation was a day of chaos. It always is. People running around trying to arrange this and that, too many people in narrow corridors carrying luggage, long queues at the purser's office to settle bills, mothers looking for their children, and husbands nursing hangovers from the previous evening's farewell parties.

Mr. Pettibone paid his bill at the purser's office taking the money to pay out of his wallet. He retrieved his envelopes from the purser's safe and then, in his cabin, he exchanged the remaining banknotes in his wallet for those in the envelope.

Mr. Pettibone knew exactly what to do. The only way to get any satisfaction, he said to himself, was to be absolutely methodical. He arranged well in advance for a car to take him to his hotel, for his luggage to be sent there directly on clearing customs, and he had bribed/tipped all and sundry lavishly to make it function smoothly. He may be working-class, but he knew how the world worked.

As they steamed into the harbour with New York to the starboard side, he ran into Mrs. Clearwater.

"Any luck?" he asked.

"No. And I still think that Major had something to do with it."

"Well, I'm sorry about it."

"Oh, don't worry. It's not worth that much, but I hate being gypped. I know it was that man."

"Well, goodbye then, madame."

"Goodbye," she said. 'What a dreadfully common little man, that Pettibone,' she thought to herself and marched off, still not on speaking terms with her husband.

A short while later in the jostling on deck, Mr. Pettibone bumped with a hard bump into the Major, almost knocking him over. They glanced at each other but passed without a word.

As he was about to leave the ship with the Major behind him, there was a commotion and he turned to see the master-at-arms running towards him. With him were two police officers who had boarded earlier with the pilot. Mr. Pettibone stopped, interested in what was about to happen. An irate Mrs. Clearwater, somewhat the worse for a glass of champagne she had just drunk when trying to make amends with her husband in their suite, was shrieking with rage.

"There he is; there's the thief. I'm sure it was him. Don't let him get away." And she pointed directly at Mr. Pettibone. His jaw dropped in surprise.

"Calm down please, madam; don't upset the other passengers. Please," said the master and they surrounded the suspect.

"Now, Sir John, we're sorry for this, but just to restore order, may I just ask you to remove your coat and hand it over?"

"Of course," said Sir John, "I've absolutely nothing to hide. And please ask that lady to stop shouting. It's attracting attention and it's very embarrassing." And so saying, he handed his camel hair coat over. From one pocket they pulled a compact envelope that contained a large wad of English five-pound notes. They called towards a small, seedy-looking man who ambled forward, took one of the notes and applied a glass to his eye. After a minute he nodded.

"What do you say about this, Sir John?" asked the master-at-arms, frankly surprised at the discovery.

"About what?"

"There have been counterfeit notes circulating on board."

"Damn me if I know anything about it."

"Well, how do you explain this?"

"I can't. They're not mine. But how they got into my pocket like that …" And his mind began to wonder.

Meanwhile, a policeman had his hand in the coat's other pocket and retrieved a silk handkerchief in which was wrapped Mrs. Clearwater's necklace.

"You see. Take me for a fool! You thought I was a stupid old fool!" she cried.

"Oh, calm down Mildred," said her husband. Taking her by the arm he led her to the gangplank.

The Major was clearly shaken and completely lost for words.

"Never seen it before. Is it that old tart's?"

"Come this way," said the police and led him back to the master-at-arm's quarters for further questioning.

During all of this, Mr. Pettibone nervously played with a coin between his fingers, making it appear and disappear. A small boy was walking past and he stopped to admire the prestidigitation. Mr. Pettibone flipped him the coin. As Sir John was led away, Mr. Pettibone heaved a slight sigh of relief.

"Absolutely first class," he said to himself as he walked down the gangplank towards the customs shed.

Chapter 2: A Small Domestic Disturbance

"You know I had quite forgotten how cold and damp the
    winters are here."
Peter von Fresheim looked at his wife with the adoration that had never
left him since the first time they met. She was everything he wanted,
and he hoped that she saw the same in him.

The baron and baroness walked down the corridor towards their
room. He would not deny that the recent years of their marriage had
been a trial. Neither of them had been perfect and each had erred in
their own way. She with other men and he …

They had now come to London, to this same hotel where they
had spent their honeymoon, seven years ago, she 20 and he 21, to try to
put things between them back in order, before they changed completely
and irretrievably.

"Nothing's changed," she said pointedly, and he mused about
whether she meant the weather or their relationship.

Taking the cigarette out of his mouth, he bent slightly and tried
to kiss her. She turned her head away.

"When we get to the room, I want you to sit down. I've
something to tell you" he said.

A sharp intake of breath and she steeled herself for more bad
news.

Taking the large brass key out of his pocket and deftly turning the lock, he opened the door and stepped aside allowing her to pass into the suite.

"This is nice," she said.

"Better than the broom cupboard we had last time," he replied.

She took her gloves off and then slowly her coat, throwing the items carelessly onto the couch to the right of the door. Glancing at herself in the mirror, she took out her hatpin and then removed the fragile concoction that was perched precariously on her head, on her golden blond hair.

"Now Peter, what did you want to tell me?" she asked turning abruptly to him. In all, he was a very handsome man, in a typical German way: tall, ramrod straight, glossy black hair, and a trim and athletic build. Funnily enough there wasn't that much Aryan blood in him. She was a true WASP, an American from New York from a very wealthy banking family. They had an arranged marriage. But it had all worked well, at least for the first few years. Until she found out …

"Let's order some tea first." And he picked up the phone and did so.

A little while later during tea, he said to her, "You know, mein Süsschen, that I would do anything for you."

She sighed and looked away.

"Well, living in Germany has been a problem for us, hasn't it? Not for me, but I know you hated the stiff conventions and the formality. Of course, my family …"

"Your family. It's always your family as you constantly remind me," she said. "Can't do this, Mama wouldn't like it; we can't move to the states because Papa relies on me to do my part like a good little German son."

Indeed, that was part of the problem. The von Fresheims owned the largest private bank in Germany. Founded as it was in the seventeenth century, it had remained in family hands ever since and prospered from generation to generation. As the oldest of four brothers, he was expected to take over from his father when the time came.

14

"Please let me finish," he insisted. "I have a surprise for you. We are leaving Germany. We are not staying in London after all. I have booked a suite for us on the Queen Mary and we shall be sailing for New York the day after tomorrow." Subconsciously, he pulled himself up on the sofa with pride at the accomplishment of a difficult undertaking. How she hated that mannerism of his; it reeked of self-righteous pomposity.

"How could you do this without asking me first? And I don't have any clothes."

"I'm afraid things had to move very quickly, and I didn't want to run the risk of your refusing to go. You see there are conditions …"

"What conditions?" She fixed him with a stare that mingled apprehension with growing delight at the prospect of leaving Germany.

"Well, I have to perform a few functions when we get to the states."

"Not for those ridiculous little men? The ones in brown shirts?"

"Not them. Better people. More refined, educated, cultured even."

"How can any Nazi be someone like that?"

"These aren't Nazis precisely. More diplomatic service."

"What exactly do you have to do?" Now she was wary.

"We get to the States, and I have taken a house on Fifth Avenue for us, complete with servants. We need to entertain, get the rich and famous to come; your father will help us, and he thinks well of Germany and Hitler. And there's no denying Hitler has done a lot for us Germans. We will be good advertisements for the Party, showing that there is no ill-will to America, that Americans and Germans really want the same thing, peace and prosperity. We need to overcome all of the negatives, the communists …"

"And the Jews?" she asked, knowing full well that his family converted to Lutheranism only two generations back.

"Well, what of it? Not all Jews of course; only those who stand in the way of the natural course and the prosperity of the country. Those who are not genuine Germans. Those who are not true patriots. But I admit these new racial purity laws are going to make things difficult even for us."

15

"It doesn't sound that you needed much convincing."

"They told me that the laws will be getting more strict next year and that they requested a special dispensation from the authorities to provide certificates for all my family, showing that while not completely pure, we are not racially tainted. That certificate has to come from a very high-up, and they said whether we get it depends on how well I do this little job for them."

"A little job? Spreading propaganda for those people!"

"It's very well paid," he said weakly.

"I suppose that makes all the difference. Aren't we rich enough?"

He paused for a moment and then very softly said, "They said that this was the only way we could get authorization to leave the country, and without it who could say what might happen. And if we do this, my parents and brothers would be allowed to leave and join us next year. If we do well."

"If we do well," she repeated. "Oh, Peter, you are such a fool. We can never do well; we never will. There will be more and more asked of us."

"Well, I can't go back now. If I did, they threatened to take over the bank for the sake of national security."

"Does your father know about this?"

"No, only that I am leaving because you can't abide the country and the people anymore. He did not quite understand. He thinks a wife should stand by her husband whatever his decision. I did say that I was only going for six months, and that I might try to see whether or not your father could help us open up a branch of the bank in New York."

"Peter, when will you stop lying? I don't think that I can take much more of this."

"Well, will you do it?"

"I'll think about it."

"You know I'm as much in love with you now as when we first met," he said.

She looked away, and a tear rolled gently out of the corner of her eye.

****

Peter opened the door of the bedroom and walked into the sitting room of the suite. The hotel staff were busily folding clothes and put them into steamer trunks and valises, with tissue paper between the creases to stop folds from forming. Amidst this, his wife was giving instructions while also talking to someone on the telephone. She seemed to become more engrossed in the conversation and then disturbed. She put the telephone down softly, and turning to the maids and the valet said gently:

"Thank you all so much. I think you need a rest. Please leave us now, and come back in half an hour."

And with that she turned back and slowly sank into the sofa, the blood drained from her face.

"Why, what is it, Liebchen?" he asked.
She didn't reply for a while and just stared ahead.

"Well?" He stood waiting.

"That was my aunt."

"Yes? Lady Harfield?"

"She said, she said …" she repeated.

"Yes?" A shudder of apprehension crept over him and he tried to fix his face into a smile. Except that the reflection in the mirror showed a grimace, an expression more of pain than pleasure.

"She said that you're as bad as her husband was. And that there is a rumour going around town that you're involved with a boy and that his mother is going to the press tomorrow as you won't stop seeing him."

"That's not true."

"Oh, don't deny it. I know all about your sordid little affairs. I've turned a blind eye because I know you do love me, and in other ways you've been a good husband. Even ignoring my flings. But this is too much. I can't stand the shame of the publicity. It will be all over town tomorrow. I won't be able to be seen in public, neither here nor in the States. So much for your little plan. Oh, why can't you control yourself? Uncle Louis was just the same. And it didn't end well."

Silence.

"I want a divorce," she said. Slowly getting up, she opened her platinum Cartier cigarette case (a gift from her father-in-law), took out a cigarette, and shakily lit it.

17

After a while, Peter got up. "I need some more cigarettes. I'm going to the tobacconist 'round the corner. When I come back ..."

"I'll be gone when you come back."

He shook his head sadly and walked out of the room.

His knees were weak as he walked, and a film of tears — or perhaps the gray mist of a London afternoon — obscured his vision. He couldn't tell. And he didn't care much. He was trying to decide whether or not he should do what Uncle Louis did, and put an end to everything. Not easy. He had the means, but did he have the courage?

As he pondered this and aimlessly turned over newspapers in the rack at the tobacconist, there was a slight cough behind him. A second cough was more insistent and he turned to see a medium-sized gentleman with a brown hat and fawn-colored overcoat.

"Peter von Fresheim? May I introduce myself? I'm a friend of your wife's aunt, Lady Harfield. Bailey's the name. Colonel Bailey. I was wondering if I could have a word?"

"Not now. It's not convenient."

"Oh, I am sorry but this is very important. I wonder if I could see you and your wife together, please."

Peter sniffed and then laughed sarcastically.

"I don't think that will be possible. In fact, I don't think she will be in."

"I think that she will want to hear what I have to say. In fact, I know she will because I have just phoned and asked her to stay in your suite and wait for us to return."

"But ...?"

"No questions, please. Let's go." And they went.

"This is a wonderful suite, Baroness. And thank you for staying to hear what I have to say. It won't take long, and I think I can be helpful. I was talking to your aunt this morning, before she phoned you, and I told her of the rumour I had heard and the slight difficulty that you may be in. I asked her to call you to let you know what was in the air ..."

"You put her up to it?" Peter's wife shouted.

"Well, I wouldn't say it quite like that," and he gave a deprecating cough. "But in my capacity, I heard about certain things that were going to happen or ... er ... could happen. I know Lady Harfield very well, from when she was married to Lord Staybrook, and

18

as I have the highest regard for your family, I thought it best if I told her, and then she could warn you."

The von Fresheims were clearly astonished and looked at each other.

"Also, I have the ... er ... fortunate ability to stop all of this from becoming public. You see if there are some things that are matters of public security — and only in such instances — I am able to force the editors of newspapers not to publish certain things, if you see what I mean."

"But this isn't a matter of public security," said Peter, "and besides there is no truth to it."

"Well, whether or not there is any truth to it, I think that your wife will agree with me if I say that should such things become public, it really would be very awkward indeed. And as to whether there is a security issue, that is really what I am here to talk to you about. Your German friends in the Abwehr are very enthusiastic about their recent recruitment and are anticipating a strong showing from you in America."

"How on earth did you find that out?"

"Well, I am very glad we've got that out of the way. It's so awkward when people deny things; don't you agree? And time-consuming, not to mention sometimes things can get, shall we say, a little unpleasant. As an Abwehr officer ..."

"No, I am in the diplomatic corps ..."

"As an Abwehr officer," the colonel continued, "you will need to supply your friends with information from time to time. Simply put, I would like to know what information you are providing. I may also have some useful information for your friends, which I would get to you in New York."

"Are you blackmailing us?" asked the Baroness.

"Such an unpleasant term, don't you think? But in a word, yes, I am blackmailing you. Let me be quite clear," he said in forthright tones. "If you don't agree to my terms, the morning papers will be full of accusations from a distraught mother. Whether or not you choose to sue is up to you, but in the meantime, the damage will have been done. People will chatter, and you will be very uncomfortable. And frankly, I don't believe you will sue, will you? You know as well as I do ... What

I want is very simple. In return for silencing this gossip, I want you to continue as you were, a happily married couple, entertain in New York, and from time to time be in contact with someone from my office. The directions will be given to you when you are settled. I assure you that there is no danger here and if you play your parts, as I know you will, you will have a wonderful time and all will be well."

"And if we don't?" asked the Baroness.

"Ah, then. You already know one consequence. The other is more serious. I shall be forced to let my discussion with you today be leaked to your Abwehr friends in Germany; the consequences will be unpleasant for your family, and I certainly could not guarantee your own safety in America. I'll be in touch. In the meantime, I wish a pleasant good day to you both."

And with that, he took up his hat, donned his coat, and strode militarily out of the suite.

The first night on an ocean liner is always dramatic. There are new people to meet, arrangements to be made, unpacking to supervise, and dinner seatings to ascertain. There is scarcely enough time for a martini before dinner. But nevertheless, with martinis in hand, Baron and Baroness von Fresheim entered the dining room of the Queen Mary, and with some obeisances were bowed to their table by the dining room manager. They were a comical lot, the other four passengers: There was a cheerful but dreadfully common man called Mr. Pettibone; a rich American couple named the Clearwaters (the husband was a banker and the Baroness made a mental note to ask whether or not he knew her father), and a rather mouldy looking English aristocrat, Sir John Cylburn-Buller. They sat down stiffly and sipped their martinis. After introductions, the common little man started to tell jokes, which were really quite amusing and seemed to all be about how he had made various terrible social gaffes. By the end of the meal, even Peter and his wife were in hysterics.

"Thank you so much for that Mr. Pettibone," Peter said. "You have quite broken the ice."

"And if I may say so, Baron, your English is impeccable quite without any trace of an accent. How come?" asked Sir John.

"I was sent to an English Boarding school, as was my father, and then I read law at King's, Cambridge."

20

"I see," said Sir John. "Well, we can't all be perfect." And he winked at Mr. Pettibone.

"By the way, Pettibone and I are going to play bridge after this. Care to join us?"

"No, no, I don't think tonight. Tomorrow perhaps."

"What about you, Mr. and Mrs. Clearwater?"

Mrs. Clearwater was about to decline the invitation, but her husband quickly said, "Mildred and I would be delighted." The game might put her in a good mood before bedtime, he thought, especially if they won.

"That's settled then. Sure you won't join us, Mr. and Mrs. Baron?" asked Sir John.

"No, thank you, but I think that we will watch for a while."

And so they did. Halfway through the last rubber, Peter said to his wife, "I want to get some fresh air. I'm just going out on deck for a few minutes."

The baroness shrugged her shoulders. "Whatever you want, Peter." she said coldly. Shortly after, she got up, excused herself, and left.

"I should say that is not a happy marriage," said Sir John and gave Mr. Pettibone a knowing look.

On deck, Peter leaned over the railing and gazed at the water. The blackness reflected his gloom. How could he have gotten himself into this position? What a fool. He turned as he heard some footsteps and saw a pleasant-looking young man approach. He felt sick. He should have looked at the passenger list, claimed to be seasick and stayed in his cabin for the duration of the journey. But it was too late now.

"Hello, Peter," said the boy. "Fancy meeting you here. Well, actually, I saw your name in the first-class passenger list and came looking for you."

"I can't say that I am pleased to see you, Piers." And the Hon Piers Roxbury shrugged his shoulders. "Well, I'm damned pleased to see you. It promised to be rather a bore but now you're here …"

"Why did you tell your mother about us? You've bloody well ruined me. In fact, you don't even know the damage you've done."

"So sorry, old boy. But you know how it is. No secrets from one's mama, eh? Besides, she's now in a tizzy because some Home Office bloke has threatened her if she goes to the press. Which is rather delightful, because it means we can start all over."

"If you think that I have even the slightest positive feeling for you ..."

"Now now, Peter, don't be angry. I am a little bored, and I have time on my hands. And when I have time on my hands my thoughts turn to love."

"You don't love me, you never did," said Peter.

"That's not true. I really do love you, Peter. I can't stop thinking about you."

"Stop it. It's over and done with."

"No, it isn't. Now look at me and tell me it isn't." And he stepped slowly towards Peter, suddenly pushing out his arms and grabbing Peter by the neck, he pressed his lips to his. He felt the resistance melt as Peter returned the embrace. Footsteps, and a cry. The two sprang apart as Peter's wife approached.

"I was just commenting to Peter what a wonderful night it was," said Piers Roxbury, and looking at his watch added, "Good Lord, is that the time? Us young'uns shouldn't be up so late. I should go to bed if I were you, Peter. Mrs. Peter, delight as always." He gave a slight bow, and somewhat tipsily walked back to the deck door and inside the ship.

"You bastard," said his wife. "I half believed you when you said it was over. Well, it's over between us now." And she took a further step towards him. He grabbed her wrists and tried to pull her towards him.

"Oh, darling, please forgive me. It won't happen again, I promise."

And she laughed bitterly, and in anger gave him a resounding slap in the face. So loud was it that it covered the sound of footsteps that suddenly stopped behind a ventilator. The deck was wet and slippery and as he was recovering from the slap, she punched him hard in the chest. Losing his balance, and with a slight cry of fright, he pitched backwards over the railings into the blackness of the night.

The footsteps retreated and the baroness could not see who made them. Had anyone observed what had just happened? She decided that she would wait this one out, and if asked would say that she was so shocked she didn't know what to do and panicked. Anyway, the ship was already well past where Peter fell and they wouldn't be able to find him. It truly was over and done with.

She went back to the cabin and waited. Nothing happened. In the morning, no one said anything, and then the next day nothing. Her husband's absences were put down to seasickness. The Hon Piers Roxbury had turned his loving attentions to someone else and had completely forgotten the incident of the kiss. On the day of disembarkation, she went to the captain.

"I'm frantic, Captain. I've searched everywhere and I can't find my husband."

"When did you find out he was missing?"

"This morning when I woke up. Well, he had been seasick the past few days and stayed mostly in our stateroom trying to sleep this off. No, he didn't ask for the doctor. Stubborn, like all Germans, he thought he could wait this out and cure it with the medicines he brought with him. Well, yesterday he was feeling a little better, but after dinner in our suite, we had a frightful row. I won't lie to you, but we have been experiencing a small domestic disturbance recently."

The captain involuntarily smiled at this charmingly old-fashioned way of putting it.

"He left me saying he would go on deck and get some air. I thought nothing of it and took my usual sleeping pill and fell asleep. A deep sleep as it happens, always so when I take those barbiturates. Anyway, when I woke up ..." And she dissolved into tears.

The ship was searched. Nothing was found. The authorities in New York were radioed and the baroness' address recorded. But it was generally felt that this was an accident, tragic indeed, but an accident nonetheless.

During the disembarkation of first-class passengers, there was a disturbance that seemed to centre on that common little man, Mr. Pettibone. But to her surprise, they were leading away the English aristocrat, Sir John Cylburn-Buller, and Mr. Pettibone made his way down the gangplank looking very pleased with himself. She drew her coat tightly around her and moving to the railing looked to see if her father was there. Seeing him, she waved, and a broad smile spread over her pretty features. Home at last; home and free. She sighed deeply with relief. Behind her, there came a slight cough.

"Man overboard, I hear," said a cultured English voice. The tone was distinctly ironic. And one she recognized. And with that, Colonel Bailey stepped back and allowed her to pass.

Chapter 3: A Brilliant Boy

You've gone up in the world haven't you, Sir?" said the page as he opened the door to the suite. "Last crossing you had an inside."

"The horses have been performing well. And don't be so fresh."

And Sir John made to cuff the page on the ear, but at the last minute handed him a gold sovereign. "Cor!" said the page recovering his balance and setting the cases down.

Sir John looked up and saw a grey-haired, trim man gazing back at him the upper lip sporting a neat military, but nicotine-stained, moustache. The eyes were stunning. Deep blue yet strangely gentle, and with more than a hint of determination. Those very eyes were responsible for all three of his marriages and, unfortunately, their termination as well. As those same eyes travelled down the mirror, he shuddered at the well-cut, but now threadbare, pinstripe, blue three-piece suit he was wearing. Yes, the horses had recently been good to him; in fact, good enough to pay for what he hoped to be his last voyage but not quite good enough that he could also face his tailor and have another wardrobe made.

As he unpacked his personal items, positioning the silver-backed, monogrammed hairbrushes precisely side by side, he reflected on the man he talked to in the train coming down from London. Despite his obvious lack of formal education and his uncouth manner, Sir John had taken a shine to him. There was something open and honest in his demeanor. Sir John reflected that he and Mr. Pettibone shared common experiences not the least of which was having to cope with reversals of fortune.

It was thoughts like these, that brought on a pang of regret. Actually, not so much a pang, more a neuralgic pain — severe, sharp and coursing through his body. A physical event, overpowering. He sat down.

"Why am I doing this?" he asked himself, and immediately there was a flashback to the meeting between him, his father, and old 'Fred,' his housemaster at Dorchester School.

"I really think that there are other ways," said Fred. "Are you sure that you need to do this?"

"Absolutely sure," said John's father. "I cannot think of any alternative."

"The school could give him a scholarship, but I am afraid given the circumstances that wouldn't cover uniforms and extracurricular expenses," said Fred.

"Well, I am sorry to say that I couldn't cover those either," said Sir Charles. "In fact, I'm completely broke, and I don't mind admitting it. My fault of course. The horses, and you remember how that was when I was a boy here?"

"Indeed, indeed."

And Dr. Warmley, nicknamed "Fred" by the boys for reasons lost in the mists of time, did remember how Charles Cylburn-Buller had run an illicit gaming group at school, how a disgruntled boy had complained about his losses and confessed to being a member, and how Charles Cylburn-Buller, although much liked and somewhat revered, had been summarily expelled.

John — all 13 years of him, slim and athletic — followed this discussion with interest, as though they were talking about someone else.

"You know, Buller, your son is absolutely brilliant. In all my 40 years here, I have never come across anyone with a similar aptitude for Maths. And a virtually photographic memory."

"I suppose the boy will make an excellent bridge player," said Sir Charles. And indeed, he did.

"I am quite sure that, if only you were able to give him a few more years, we would be able to get him into Oxford or even, perish the thought, Cambridge, and he would do very well."

26

"I am sorry," said Sir Charles. "It's really no-go."

And so, John's father withdrew him from Dorchester in his third term and he entered the local grammar school as a scholarship boy. He did very well there, and although he was not generally liked at first because of his posh manner, he did his best to be affable. By the time he was in the sixth form, his good humor and easy-going ways endeared him to his peers. That and his amazing ability to lie. Despite his best intentions, he could not resist embellishing stories about himself to the extent that the headmaster had pulled him aside one day and said:

"You know, John, you really don't need to tell all those tall tales. You're quite exceptional enough."

"But, Sir, it's the only way I can hold the boys' attention," he explained.

With Fred's help and coaching during the school holidays, he was able to win a scholarship to Cardinal College, Oxford. Supplemented by his winnings at cards, his first term went rather well. He amassed large sums from people in London clubs who had invited Sir Charles' only son and heir out for an occasional dinner. By the second term, things were going even better and his tutor was impressed by his ability and application.

"You know, Mr. Cylburn-Buller, I wouldn't be surprised if you got a first in Honours Mods," he said. And indeed, he did.

But then came the war. The War to End All Wars it was called, and he was called up in 1917. On the whole, he had a good war, if such may be said, rapidly being promoted from subaltern to captain, and then eventually, major. His courage was undisputed, and he was awarded both an MC and the DSO. Or he would have been if his lying hadn't got in the way. Lt. Colonel Bailey, his commanding officer, noticed certain discrepancies in the mess accounts, for which John was responsible, and when confronted, John covered his peculation with an amazing concoction of lies that even he did not believe.

"You know, Buller," said the colonel, "I would have let you off if you would have admitted this. We would have put it down to stress, war-weariness, an error of judgment or some such. You really are one of my best officers. But if there's one thing I can't abide, it's a lie."

"Yes, Sir," said John dismally.

"I think that we will keep this between ourselves, and I want to give you a second chance. So, I won't do what would normally be done … request your demotion to the ranks or even a court-martial. But I am going to rescind my recommendations for the MC and DSO. And I shall keep a very close eye on you from now on."

And he did for the next nine months, until early in 1918 John was severely wounded during the fourth battle of Ypres and shipped back to Britain. His recovery was slow, and not all the shrapnel was removed, leaving him with a limp and various aches and pains. But the damage was more to his mind than anything, and took three years with Dr. Rivers in Scotland following rounds of electro-therapy, and eventually he had all but recovered. His finances, however, had not.

His father died during the war, leaving John with a baronetcy and colossal debts. The estate and house in Belgravia had been sold to partially cover these and there was nothing left. On discharge from Craiglockhart Military Hospital, he pondered over his career and tried various things: teaching at preparatory schools and a brief spell as a stockbroker in the city. But it was all too boring, even though his aptitude with numbers and his memory made him excel in each endeavor. His heart just wasn't in it.

He lacked concentration in everything except playing cards. He could do this for hours on end. And so he had embarked on his career of choice, traveling backwards and forwards across the Atlantic playing cards with those willing to lose large amounts of cash. He had been generally very successful, winning more than he lost, and was slowly paying off the remainder of his father's debts.

Not that he was a cardsharp; no, his dealings were always on the up and up. So it was that despite the occasional complaint and the scrutiny of pursers and masters-at-arms on the Berengaria, Olympic and Aquitania, nothing could be brought against him and he was allowed to pursue his chosen career, unhindered. And now he hoped this voyage, on the new Queen Mary, would be the last. He would continue to win, he knew, and then settle in the States, and invest in … well, something, with his winnings. He had always admired Americans and had made good friends with one or two Rhodes Scholars when at Oxford; his aim was to meet up with them once in New York and see whether there was something they could offer him. It was time to settle down and put those three marriages behind him. At 43 he was still attractive, or so he thought, and he was sure that he could find a rich American widow, either on board or in the States. All ladies loved him for his blue eyes, his charm and — for the Americans — his splendid English accent. Except for his hair, which had turned white during the war, and perhaps the nicotine-staining of his mustache, and the shabbiness of his clothes, he still was very presentable. And so he straightened himself, and with as much of a military bearing as the shrapnel wounds would allow (they were behaving themselves tonight), he strode across the first-class dining room to his table.

They were not a very inspiring lot, his fellow passengers. There was that odd little man, Mr. Pettibone, who nodded affably to him as he sat down next to him. Oh, why had he given Pettibone his card? Overcome with sentimental camaraderie, he thought, but how foolish. No doubt he would have to spend some time avoiding him during this journey.

Then there were the two Germans, not a happily married couple he observed, and the American couple. The Germans were odd, though; she was clearly an American and he spoke impeccable English. Could they be imposters? He chose his meal carefully, and after introducing himself, he pondered what he could do to cheer up the table. But in a short while, he knew he didn't need to bother. Mr. Pettibone had everyone in stitches, even the Germans, whose stiff facial expressions had softened slightly, but still, they did not look at each other. Towards the end of the dinner, he invited the group to play bridge, and with foresight he had slipped the smoking room steward a fiver to keep two tables permanently at his call. The Germans refused, so it was him, the Americans and Pettibone. The game went well and he and Mr. Pettibone as partners ended up winning a surprisingly large amount from the Clearwaters. Mrs. C. looked at him with a sharp and fierce expression, and she was clearly about to say something rather rude, when Mr. C. stood up and said:

"Time for your pills, Mildred," and led her away by the elbow, but not before she said to Sir John:

"You know, there's something not quite right about you."

Mr. Clearwater, coloured with embarrassment, apologized. "No," she said. "I shan't apologize, I mean it. That man's a crook. I don't go for that smarmy style. All put on," she said. All of this was spoken loudly as the mortified Mr. Clearwater steered his wife from the room. Clearly, John's lovely blue eyes had not worked their magic on Mrs. C.

The next morning, Sir John summoned his steward and arranged for drinks, cigars and,canapés together with the full services of staff for his suite starting at 3:30 p.m. Scanning through the passenger list, he saw two old friends from the war were in the first-class section: Colonel Bailey, his old commanding officer, and Lord Staybrook (who had been another company commander in his regiment). Undaunted, he approached them, and after a few drinks they agreed to play cards with him, as did Mr. Pettibone, who appeared to need little persuasion when told that a peer would be present.

Colonel Bailey however, needed some effort, but eventually agreed to at least play for a short while. Lord Staybrook was a sporting man. Colonel Bailey's manner struck Sir John as being like that of a surgeon approaching an unpleasant but fascinating operation. He had the distinct impression that the colonel wanted to see whether or not John was on the straight and narrow; and if he wasn't, well he wasn't sure that the colonel would give him another chance. But the fact was that he was indeed on the straight and narrow. It was just that he was so very good at cards: He could memorize them, mentally count them out and do amazing statistical analysis all in his head. And he usually won. And he did that afternoon. Lord Staybrook in his good-natured way, laughed at his losses, while Colonel Bailey shook his head saying in a not-too-friendly way, "I don't know how you do it." But it was Mr. Pettibone who seemed the most put out, but nonetheless paid up. In cash, no IOU. Despite this, Pettibone had agreed the following day to a second game with Sir John and Lord Staybrook.

When they all had left after that second meeting, John took out the banknotes and looked at them. He had been highly amused by Mr. Pettibone's somewhat crass attempts to explain the various fraud-preventing measures used by the Bank of England. What could that little man know about forged banknotes? No doubt something he had read in the *News of the World*, despite his explanation of being some sort of accountant. A turf accountant, no doubt. Taking a close look at the notes, just for a lark, his blue eyes opened wide, and he put that note down. He took another, and then another up and sequentially laid them down. All of these came from Pettibone. He examined those from the colonel. Lord Staybrook had given him an IOU.

He took out his forty-third cigarette of the day and lighting it exclaimed:

"Jesus Christ, that old bastard!"

In his line of business, Sir John was also intimately acquainted with the vagaries of British high-value banknotes. But what to do? He could of course remonstrate with Pettibone; but what would he say? "Very sorry. Don't know the first thing about it." "But you are supposed to know about these things," John might say. "Oh that," Pettibone would likely reply. "Just talk to amuse the ladies." And he might say that, or he might not. And John stomped around the living room of his suite desperately trying to make up his mind what to do.

At dinner that evening seated next to Mr. Pettibone, he tried to engage him in conversation, but Mr. Pettibone was having none of it and turned his attentions to the baroness, who was sitting next to him. After dinner, John tried to get Mr. Pettibone to play cards with him.

"What? After my losses, not on your Nellie," he said, and laughed a good-humored laugh. "No hard feelings, but …"

And Sir John went away. Clearly Mr. Pettibone had come up with a wonderful method of laundering his money. Later that night, after a few stiff whiskies, he saw Mr. Pettibone across the room. He stood up; now the pieces of shrapnel were giving him hell, and he was not in the mood for niceties. Walking up to him, he spun Pettibone 'round and in a rasping whisper said:

"What I can't make out, Pettibone, is this: Did you print those notes yourself or did you have someone else do it?"

Shaking himself free, and with a gracefulness of which few would have thought him capable, Pettibone said, "I don't know what you're talking about. Those notes were first class, absolutely first class. Came from a client, titled, impeccable." And he was about to walk away.

"You know, Pettibone," Sir John said, "I could really help you. I think that we could make an excellent team."

Mr. Pettibone shook his head slowly and with a sad smile tapped his head with his right forefinger.

"You know what? You're absolutely batty, my friend. And you're drunk. My advice? As my old dad said: Sleep it off, why don't you?"

And with that, Mr. Pettibone walked away

31

Chapter 4: If t'were Done

He stopped his unpacking and considered. He really didn't know exactly when he knew … when he knew that he had to kill her. Walter Clearwater regarded his wife as she was carefully unpacking the steamer trunks that the stewards had delivered to their suite.

"Which side do you want?"

"I don't mind," he said. "Which would you prefer?"

"For God's sake, can't you even make up your mind about this? Do I have to do everything?"

He sighed. "The right side. The right side and the top two drawers of that thing there and the left side of the closet."

"Why do you need to take up so much space? You know I've brought all these clothes. Worth, Chanel, Dior, and they need room. You men can look the same every day and no one cares. I know I don't, well not about you anyway." And she glanced at her paunchy, bald husband and tried to remember what he had looked like in his youth. The effort was not successful.

"Okay, Mildred, whatever you say, whatever you want." And he went on with his unpacking and his musing.

The problem had started a year ago. Normally a placid and very careful woman, there had been a significant change in her personality. It began with her accusing the servants of stealing small items: a cheap cigarette box, a paltry porcelain vase. That sort of thing. Of course, it was nothing of the sort. The new maid had simply put them in a different place.

Then it was her watch: That one was difficult. She summoned the staff, then the cops, and it ended with one of the maids being dragged off in handcuffs and hysterical tears. The watch had fallen behind a table; he found it later, put it back and squared things with the police and ultimately with the maid. But that had cost him a lot of money. And if there was something that Walter Clearwater didn't like, it was spending money. Except when it came to his wife, that is; for he had loved her for every minute of their 27-year marriage.

Then came the accusations that he was having an affair: with his secretary, with the daughter of the chauffeur, with their best friend's wife. Actually, nothing of the sort; he had been faithful for every day of their marriage. Not that there hadn't been temptations. Looking at him now, he thought, who but Mildred could still want him? Although with his wealth and position a dalliance was not an impossibility. But 20 years ago … well, 20 years ago he was young, slim, energetic and had his impeccable hair. All of that had gone, but not his smile. Still very engaging and when he did smile, well anything could have happened … but it didn't. And he had very little to smile about these days.

Mildred had phoned up his partners at the bank, saying that they needed to know.

"To know what?" they had asked.

She told them that Walter was being very secretive these days, hiding things and now was spending large sums although she didn't know on what, and those affairs, well they must be costly. Of course, she didn't care. She only had their friendship in mind, and naturally the welfare and standing of the bank. Did they think that things were alright at the bank? Were funds missing? She thought it unlikely, but perhaps it would be good to check. And with a shake of their collective heads, check they did.

They called in an auditor and as much as they tried to keep that silent, somehow it got out. The press got wind, and then the authorities came in to examine the books. Clients were getting edgy, and as much as Clearwater and his partners and staff tried to reassure them nothing was amiss — and nothing was amiss in truth — the panic had already started. The bank's stability was questioned and daily the financial position sank until it finally reached a very disturbing level. At that point, Fresheim Sohne, the German bank, always on the lookout for a bargain, made an offer, a derisory one. But even so, the partners were tempted to accept, not wishing to face any more scrutiny.,

Clearwater, the senior partner and principal stockholder, knew that there was nothing wrong and that the bank just needed to weather the storm. He decided to go to Europe and persuade old Baron von Fresheim to withdraw the offer, although he was aware that in the short term that would make things worse. And he had not succeeded. And in a sour mood, he and Mildred had progressed back from Cologne, through Paris and London, where at Claridges they had briefly run into von Fresheim's son and his American wife.

"Something odd about that couple," Mildred said. But she was always saying nasty things nowadays. Especially about people, and even more so about her relatives. He picked up the bottle of pills that her idiot of a doctor prescribed to calm her nerves and help her sleep. All it did was make her even more unpleasant and groggy on top of it. Three of those damned things would put her into a deep sleep at night, and she would lie on her back and snore like tortured bagpipes keeping him awake. He needed his sleep; he needed to think how he was going to get out of this mess, a mess that she had created. In sickness and in health, 'til death do us part. Well, he was going to do his part; he opened the top drawer of the trunk and took out a dark glass bottle that contained the pills he gave her every evening. She relied on him.

"You know, Walter, I don't know what I would do without you," she had said yesterday evening. I rely on you so much. You're such a good husband and I know I have been bad these past few months. I don't know what is wrong with me." And she reached out and clutched his arm. "You won't leave me, will you? Will you?" She pleaded: "I love you so much; life without you wouldn't be life. I will be better, I promise, only don't leave, don't leave." And she drew him near to her and her eyes were so imploring, so beseeching. And in a flash, he saw her as she was when he first married her. Stunningly beautiful, long auburn hair, and a figure, well *that* figure, breathtaking and so intelligent, and above all so very, very kind. Her eyes sought his and there was such appeal to him, a prayer. And his heart melted.

But today, well, today was no different than any of the others in the recent past. Yesterday evening was forgotten and today was …

"What the hell did you do with my pearls, Walter? Where are they? Are you holding them back from me so that you can sell them when we get back to New York, to save that rubbish bank of yours? I know what you've been up to. You can't fool me, oh, no."

"Mildred," he said mildly, "you gave them to the purser for safekeeping, remember?"

"Oh, oh, so I did. Well, never mind. I know what you're thinking. Remember that." And she threw down the dress she was carrying and fled to the bedroom, slamming the door with a loud bang. Walter clutched at the pill bottle and put it slowly in his pocket.

At dinner that night, the same group were there as on the previous evening. That odious little man, Mr. Pettibone, the von Fresheims and Sir John something-or-the-other.

"Mr. Pettibone, what is it exactly that you do?" Mildred asked pointedly, apropos of nothing in particular.

Taken aback, he replied, "Well, Madame, as I said yesterday, I'm a type of accountant."

"What type? All the accountants I know are crooks and several of them are behind bars. Are you a crook, Mr. Pettibone?"

And Mr. Pettibone, good-natured as always, laughed and laughed until he turned purple and coughed. Sir John gave him a glass of water and patted him on the back.

"Mildred!" said her husband.

"Shut up, Walter," she said. "Oh, you don't know my husband, do you? Well, not like I do. If ever there was a fraud, it's him. Do you know what he did at his bank? You won't believe …"

A hush fell on the table and all eyes were on her. Pale and trembling, Walter stood up. "I'm so very sorry ladies and gentlemen; please forgive us, but my wife hasn't been too well lately." Mildred had fallen into a sort of trance and was gazing off into the distance, her anger spent. Very, very gently he put his hand under her arm and slowly eased her up out of her chair.

"Mildred, my love, it's really time for us to turn in."

And she looked at the group. "Goodnight, everyone," she broke into a radiant smile. "It's been such a pleasant evening." And there was no hint of irony in her voice.

Colonel Bailey at the next table saw all this and turning to his companion said, "That lady is clearly ill. I wonder whether I can help?"

Mid-morning in the first-class lounge, Mr. and Mrs. Clearwater were sitting side by side in comfortable armchairs, looking the very picture of wealth at ease. The colonel walked up slowly and asked whether he could sit with them. Reluctantly they agreed. Turning to her husband, Mildred asked, "Who is this old bore? Do you know him, Walter?" Mr. Clearwater looked at Colonel Bailey with a sad expression but did not say anything. The colonel ignored the question and obviously in an excellent mood he laughed and asked, "Do you live in New York?" He continued. "It will be my first time in that city. I have heard so much about it and I've always wanted to go. And now I shall. I can't conceal from you that I am very excited. This will positively be my last trip and I would so like to make it a memorable one. If it's not too much of an imposition, could you recommend a few things that I must do and see when I get there?"

"Well, we do have a place in New York, but we mainly live in Westchester. You must visit us," said Mildred, warming instantly to the colonel, as he intended. "But why your last trip?"

"Oh, yes, positively my last. In fact, this is a one-way ticket. I shan't be going back."

"Do you intend to live in the States?"

"Oh, no. My visit will be very brief I am sure, but I do want to cram in some sightseeing before I go."

"But …?" asked Mildred, puzzled by this.

"Coffee? Mildred, coffee?"

"Yes, dear."

"Colonel?"

"No, not for me thanks."

And Walter walked off. Colonel Bailey watched him at the counter collecting Mildred's coffee. He saw Clearwater take something out of his pocket, but because he had turned his back, he wasn't sure what was happening. Probably putting some sugar into the coffee.

"Mrs. Clearwater, do you take sugar?"

"No, only some sort of sweetener. It's a special kind that Walter gets for me. You can't buy it in the stores. It's very sweet, just like me," she simpered.

"Well, that must be it," he thought. But just to be sure …

"Mr. Clearwater, how nice of you, but I have quite changed my mind." And Colonel Bailey took the cup of coffee from Walter's hand before he could say anything.

'Bitter,' he thought on taking a small sip. 'Definitely not sweetener. Surely even Mildred would have noticed this clumsy attempt or whatever it was. But if she were to complain, no one would have believed her. Very clever.'

"I'm so sorry, Mrs. Clearwater. I had forgotten my manners," he said and looked pointedly at Walter, shaking his head almost imperceptibly from side to side. "Please allow me to get you another cup."

"I don't want it, thanks all the same," she said. Not now anyway," and stared off into space.

That evening at dinner, the Clearwaters were silent. Afterwards, as they were getting up, Bailey turned to Walter and quietly said, "You look a little peaky. A spell on deck will do you good."

"I'm okay, really okay. Kind of you though."

"No, you need some air. And," he whispered, "I have something important to say to you."

Walter made his excuses, and Mildred, looking suspicious, said, "Don't be long, Walter. I want a good night's rest. And I need those pills. So hurry back."

"Right you are," he said and followed the colonel out of the dining room.

"Well, what is it?" It was cold and there was quite a breeze.

"Over here," said the colonel. "Let's get out of this wind. Now I don't know what you are planning, and …"

"What on earth are you talking about?" asked Walter.

"I think you know. Besides, time is short; I'm cold and I don't want to draw this out."

"What the hell are you on about?" Walter was angry.

"It's like this. Are you sure you can do it? I mean really do it. Can you live with the regret? The consciousness of what you have done? You have no idea what it's like, and if you think that prison is bad — a physical prison, that is — you can't possibly imagine what a prison you make for yourself in your mind is like."

Walter stared at him.

"I know because I've been there. And my life has been hell, damned hell ever since."

"What do you mean?"

"During the war, when I was a captain leading a company of 200 men. Doesn't matter which regiment, what division, or where. We were in the trenches in a forward position, with the Germans 200 yards away. Heavy fortified position with machine-gun emplacements. Three days before, we were given the order to reconnoitre at night. Stake out the wire and listen to any talking in the lines so that we could have some info about the next wave … if we could get close. I chose one of my subalterns, a young boy just out of school. Eighteen, eager, and very keen to prove himself. I knew he could speak some German, and I told him to get out when he wanted and take three men with him. Crawl out and if possible, take a prisoner. I should have chosen someone a little older, or gone myself, but I didn't. I don't know why. No moon that night. Well, for some reason the Germans were edgy and a flare went up and caught the group just when they were halfway over to them, and I heard the spitting patter of the machine guns as they opened up. My subaltern crawled back eventually, completely unscathed.

'Where are the others?' I asked.

'Dead, Sir' he stammered. 'Didn't stand a chance.'

"And he stood in front of me shaking with fear, with death in his eyes.

'Bad luck,' I said, and told him to go to the dugout, and I got his sergeant to give him a good tot of whiskey."

"Yes, yes, all very nice," said Walter. "Do let's share war stories sometime. But what on earth has this to do with me?" he asked irritated.

"So the next day, this fledgling was still a bundle of nerves, and had that thousand-yard stare that we now know is shell-shock. Anyway, we were short of men, sustained many losses, and I could not have this. Fear is contagious.

'Damn you, Scott,' I said. 'Pull yourself together. You've got to lead your platoon and we'll get the order to go over any day.'

'I can't go, Sir.'

'What do you mean you can't go?'

'I can't go.'

'Do you know that I can court-martial you on the spot for that? In fact, cowardice in the face of the enemy means a firing squad. Either way you'll face death. Do you want to die a hero or a coward?'"

The colonel continued, "I thought that would buck him up. It didn't."

Walter yawned a drawn-out yawn and looked at his watch.

"At 4 a.m. the order came to go over the top. I blew my whistle, and my lieutenants on the left lunged forward while Scott stood there. 'Blow your whistle, damn you,' I bellowed.

"The troops were going over the top. The machine gun batteries were starting up, flares were sent, and the ring and whirr of shrapnel was all around. 'Get up,' I said, and I tried to push him up the wall of the trench. He shrank back and sat down. The men about to go over hesitated and looked at him.

'Sergeant,' I said. 'This man has a fever and is very ill. Take him to the medical officer.'"

The colonel was too far into the story to stop now. "I was one of the few survivors that day. We lost some truly first-rate men. It's like losing a close family member, a brother. I ordered Scott to be guarded and I wrote to my CO. Within a day, the request came back for me to convene a firing squad. No one wanted to be a part of this, myself included. Scott was well-liked and rather a mascot. I promised my men extra rations and booze, and then demanded that six of them appear at 6 a.m. with their rifles. 'Yes, Sir' was the sullen response. But I knew they would be there. Good men.

"I visited Scott guarded in the officer's dugout and sent all away except for Scott and the duty sergeant. It was pitch-black outside, there was desultory firing in the background, but nothing much to speak of. Lit only by candles, I still saw Scott's pale face. He looked so very young and innocent. I put the bottle of whiskey down.

'They're going to shoot me tomorrow, Sir?'
'Yes.'
'Will they tell my mother? About me I mean?'
'I don't know.'

"And he broke down and put his head in his hands and cried his heart out. The long, dirty blond hair streamed over his hands and the shadows broadened over his head.

'Have another?' I said to him and poured him a full tumbler.

39

"After several, we were both tipsy.

'I wonder what death is like, Sir?' he asked.

'I don't know. I haven't tried it.'

"Slowly I took out my Webley service revolver and placed it on the table. He looked at it, and then at me. The expression was one that I cannot describe really and will never forget. There was no fear, but there was pity and pain and regret and innocence all combined.

'Sergeant,' I said. "Go and get us another bottle.'

'But, Sir. You haven't finished this one.'

'Go!'

'Yes, Sir.'

"Once the sergeant left, I picked up the revolver. I gently put Scott's right hand around it, covering it with my own and drew back the firing pin."

'For God, King and country,' I said.

'For God ...' he replied, but could not complete the sentence.

'Are you ready?' I asked.

'Yes, Sir,' he said and he looked me straight in the eye. I pulled the trigger."

"The sergeant came running back and looked at the scene with horror.

'Lieutenant Scott appears to have had an accident, Sergeant. You can call off the firing squad.'

"And so I killed this boy, and it's no use saying, Well, he would have died anyway. Because cruelly, I survived; and I feel him there, in front of me now, and every night and on and on for the past 20 years. I can't escape it. The remorse. Could you?"

And Walter looked at him horrified.

"Well, good night, Mr. Clearwater. It's time for my bed."

Walter walked to the railing and stared at the fast-moving blackness below. He reached into his pocket and threw out the bottle, and it shattered as it broke against the hull of the boat in its descent.

Chapter 5: Journey's End

"Journeys end in lovers meeting,
Every wise man's son doth know"

Shakespeare, *Twelfth Night*

Colonel Bailey lay on the examination couch as Dr. Feathers' deft hands palpated. From the left side of the abdomen to the right, and slowly down to the suprapubic area, exploring and gathering information from his fingertips.

"And the headaches, how long have you been having these, Colonel?"

"Oh, about a month."

"Changing in any way?"

"Oh, just a little more frequent," he replied. "They wake me at night sometimes, and I occasionally feel a little sick with them but it goes."

"Any change in your eyesight?"

"Not much, a little blurry perhaps."

"Hmm," said the doctor.

Colonel Bailey liked the doctor, and the doctor liked him.

"Please sit up, Sir."

And the RAMC captain looked into his eyes with the ophthalmoscope and noted the early signs of papilledema.

"You can get dressed now, Sir."

"Well, Captain, what's the damage?"

The captain looked embarrassed.

"How long?"

The captain was disturbed, clearly.

"Should I start reading a long novel, say *War and Peace*?"

The captain forced a wry smile. "Not if you want to finish it, Sir," he said.

"I see. Then I better start making plans."

"I will give you some medications. Some you can take by mouth, but when the pain becomes bad you will need to inject. Will you be able to do it?"

Bailey laughed. "Of course," and he took the black leather case containing the syringes and the prescription. The captain saluted, and Bailey left the room.

Things had been getting worse lately, and the dull ache in his back was no laughing matter. Except he did laugh; wasn't life funny after all? He asked Scott about it. Odd, Scott had been even more on his mind lately but it was only recently that he had actually begun to see and hear him. Just a shadowy presence, at first, at dusk, out of the corner of his eye. A fleeting presence and then gone. But each time he was there, Bailey felt a strange peace. He relaxed.

"Well, Scott?" he asked.

"Sir?" the young man replied.

"What's it like?"

"Couldn't really say," was the reply. And Colonel Bailey left it at that.

Colonel Bailey had always wanted to go to New York. The American captain — Shawe was his name — with whom he had liaised in 1918 had told him all about it. Of course, some belief had to be suspended, as Shawe was a New Yorker, and everything looks so much rosier when you are separated and far from those things and people you love. And when you might very shortly die. And when you will very shortly die, Bailey repeated and chuckled to himself. He wanted to ask Scott some more, but Scott had gone.

The mild rocking to and fro of the ship as it navigated the Atlantic felt very soothing. Except to those who were seasick. Bailey was inclined to seasickness. He had begun to increase the morphia injections to control the pain as it worsened, and this had curiously also helped with his nausea. He bumped into Sir John Cylburn-Buller in the bar.

"Haven't seen you for years," said John, known to many simply as the Major. "Buy you a drink?"

"Yes, scotch and soda," Bailey replied.

And they chatted and talked and caught up. John's story distressed the colonel, who had thought very highly of him as an officer under his command. Brave man, he remembered. Why hadn't he settled down? Of course, there was that less savory side to his character, he mused as he remembered the questionable incident of the mess accounts and his agony over rescinding the recommendation for the bravery medals. But he did not want to ask further, as he listened to John's litany of debts, woe, and indiscretions. Shell shock. It had to be. Changed men for life, he reasoned. Bailey wondered why he hadn't succumbed; he had no signs of it, or so he thought, and had continued with his commission in the Staybrookshire Regiment and then Military Intelligence without any concerns after the war. Except remorse, which like a shadow, he couldn't shake off and that did not disappear in the dark.

"I can't absolve you," said the colonel.

"I don't need absolution," replied John.

"I do," said the colonel, and he got up.

"You loved us, didn't you? All of us. Like family, like …"

"You can't possibly know how much," said Colonel Bailey, and he left.

****

At Sir John's insistence, Bailey went to a card game in his suite, and there he met that comical little fellow Pettibone. Instantly taking a liking to him, they chatted for a while in between hands, and the colonel noticed how carefully Pettibone handled cash, deftly exchanging notes from his wallet with those of his winnings and carefully keeping them separate. 'Interesting,' thought Bailey. 'I wonder what he is up to?'

"By the way," said Bailey, "I noticed that odd American lady this morning. She had a shouting match with her husband in the corridor outside my cabin. You could probably hear the row in Penzance. Do you know her?"

Sir John laughed. "Oh, her. She's quite sharp but a little batty. I've grown rather fond of her."

"I think she is ill," said Bailey." I think she might have a brain tumour. You know that can make you do or see some very odd things."

"You don't say," said Sir John.

When a disgruntled Pettibone got up to go after clearly losing more than he could afford, Bailey got up with him and walked him to the door.

"Be careful," was all he said.

Pettibone stared at him.

"Be careful," Bailey repeated and saw him out.

The following day, quite coincidentally it appeared, Bailey came across the Clearwaters in the first-class lounge. It was evident to him that there were serious problems here. He thought it important to have a word, to warn Clearwater of any folly, just as he had warned Pettibone.

"Those pills that I take, they make things so clear to me. I wonder why that is? Everything seems so sharp and in focus" he mused.

"Sometimes death will do that, Sir," said Scott, who was evidently behind him.

"But I'm not dead," said Bailey.

"What was that?" asked Clearwater responding to Bailey's mumbling.

And later that night he had a word with Clearwater. He didn't know what Clearwater would do, or if he had made any difference at all, but he had done what he needed. He rounded the corner of the deckhouse and as he paused behind a ventilator heard a slight cry but saw nothing. Nothing at all. Or had he? Then came the splash.

"She's done him in, Sir," said Scott boyishly and giggled.

"Don't be daft," said Colonel Bailey, and he went to bed.

The next day, he considered what he thought he had seen and heard. But these days he could not count on his senses. Probably the medication, and …

He went for a walk on deck, and there saw a disconsolate Baroness von Fresheim.

"Gruss Gott," he said.

"What?" she replied.

"Oh, you don't speak German then?" he said sarcastically.

"It's you," she recognized him and started to walk away.

"Where's your husband? I really would like a word."

"He's not well. And besides, I don't think he will want to see you."

"That's as may be, but you remember our little agreement. You and your husband would let me know what the Germans are up to in New York in return for the rumours of his indiscretions to be silenced. I've kept my side of the bargain. Perhaps naive of me, but I would really like you to keep yours."

"Another threat, Colonel? You really are a despicable man."

Bailey thought for a moment. "You don't know how right you are. By the way, was it you I saw on deck yesterday, very late?"

"No."

"I could have sworn I smelled your perfume."

"No, you're quite mistaken."

Scott said, "She did it, Sir. She pushed him over. You could use that you know. Something to hold over her, and she could prove to be very useful to us."

Bailey did not reply.

For the next few days, he kept a very close eye on her, hoping to see her husband. But to no avail. He questioned, discretely of course, the stewards and dining room staff. They had not seen Fresheim either. He was always in bed or somewhere undisclosed on deck when they needed to interact with him, always 'alibius,' somewhere else. Anyway, it wasn't their job to babysit the passengers and besides, his wife appeared to be taking good care of him. They hinted that it was no business of theirs, or of the colonel's either come to that.

45

If Fresheim were dead the loss would be a wasted opportunity and difficult to explain to his masters at the ministry. But there was more to it than that, much more. Bailey's conscience would not let it go. Not again, and not this time. And time for him was short. "That damned conscience, it doth make cowards of us," he quoted Shakespeare maladroitly. He reasoned we were well past the point where, or if, he had gone overboard. They would never find him. It would be too late now anyway. And if he had disappeared, as Scott seemed to think, how could she so reasonably explain his absence? But at heart he felt he should go to the ship's captain and let him make the decision. But he didn't.

On the day of disembarkation, troubled in mind, body and spirit, and feeling very ill, he ventured on deck. His kit was packed. He had taken an extra couple of injections just before and was weary.

He coughed as he came up behind the Baroness. She really was looking radiant as she was about to go down the gangplank.

"Man overboard, I hear," he whispered.

Bailey suddenly realized he was feeling too ill and feeble to disembark himself, just yet, and decided to go back to his suite for a rest before the ordeals at immigration and customs.

On opening the suite door, and then gently closing it behind him, he was aware that his right hand was weak, and he had trouble with the lock.

"I'm sorry, Sir," said Scott from a chair in the corner of the room. "Sorry about the trouble I caused you. In the war, I mean. And now with what I said about the baroness and her husband."

"That's okay," said Bailey. "I know you couldn't help it."

"I don't think you should get involved with things that don't concern you, Sir. The baroness and everything," said the young man.

"Don't know why you care about me. You shouldn't you know. Besides, isn't it important to do the right thing? Otherwise, what are we here for?"

"Couldn't tell you, Sir. And it isn't always clear what the right thing might be. For example, some may say you did the right thing back then." And he motioned to the drawer where Bailey kept his service revolver.

"Do you?"

No answer.

"For God's sake, Scott, answer me," he implored. "Answer me … Christopher, please. Please!"

But his words were not uttered, as he no longer had a voice. Not anymore.

"Damn," he thought, and got up. Should he call on the doctor? He pondered this. "No, I've had enough, and he took the revolver out of the drawer. But it was too heavy for him, and he dropped it with a dull thud. The safety catch was on, and it did not fire. No fire left, he laughed mirthlessly, except the fires of Hell.

"Go back to bed, Sir," said Scott gently.

And Bailey did what he was told.

"I don't suppose I'll see New York now," Bailey lamented.

"No, Sir."

"Well, it's goodbye to all that, I suppose."

Scott handed him the black leather case. Almost with loving affection, his hands caressed the soft leather. Scott opened the case, and Bailey drew up a large draft of morphia into the barrel of the syringe.

"Goodbye, Scott."

"Hello, Sir. I'll be seeing you."

As Bailey pushed the plunger down sharply, he could feel the warmth entering his veins, and with a calm sigh he turned his head, and sank into the everlasting.

Part II: Mr. Pettibone to the Rescue

Chapter 1: A Most Valued Possession

Mr. Pettibone gazed at his reflection as much as he could from his position in front of the shop window. He had lost his paunch and was so much slimmer than before the war. Although the tailor adapted his clothes to cope with the change, Mr. Pettibone's skin hadn't and hung in loose folds about his neck and lips, making him look jowly and a little dejected. That belied his character, which was as jovial as ever. The world was still a source of joy to him, even after his five-year stint in Wormwood Scrubs. Five years for debasing the currency — in other words, printing and passing counterfeit banknotes. They were very good ones, and he had taken pride in his work. Five years of his life, but it certainly could have been a lot longer. A fit of remorse overcame him when he disembarked from the Queen Mary in New York that February in 1937. Major Sir John Cylburn-Buller had been kind to him on that voyage, and he had returned the favor by planting the notes and the stolen necklace on him.

"Shame on you, Bert." He heard in his mind, his dear old dad say, "You're a disgrace to the family."

And so he had gone to the Police Precinct and confessed. The Major had been released and Mr. Pettibone deported from America back to England. Then the trial. Then prison. Then the war. He volunteered to do his bit and was sent to be part of an anti-aircraft battery unit on the South Coast. What with the war and rationing, well it had been impossible to keep his figure in good order and so he had lost much weight.

49

While in prison, he had pondered what to do to turn an honest penny when he got out. And one Sunday when he was seated reluctantly in the prison chapel, and when he should have been paying attention to the sermon, it suddenly came to him: open up an antiques shop specializing in paintings and furniture.

'You have the eye, my boy,' he said to himself. 'You certainly have the eye. A good counterfeiter must.' He frowned at the thought of his past misdeeds. And borrowing some money from a few former colleagues — most of whom shared a similar interesting background to that of Mr. Pettibone and who owed him many favours — he opened Pettibone, Sons and Langford, Dealers and Valuers of Fine Antiques. In truth, there were no sons, and certainly no Langford, but he thought that it gave the store an aura of respectability. So now here he was after a few weeks in business, standing outside his shop located on a side road off Bond Street in London, in the rain and staring at himself in the window.

Admiring a Chippendale sideboard that he had tastefully arranged together with a matching table and chairs to the right in the window, he heard a sharp intake of breath behind him.

"Upon my soul, it's that old rogue, Pettibone. How are you? Is this your place?"

Major Sir John Cylburn-Buller advanced towards him with an outstretched hand, which Pettibone eagerly took and shook.

"Major, absolutely first class to see you again. I hope that there are no hard feelings?" And Mr. Pettibone's erstwhile chins wobbled with unfeigned delight.

"None, really. You put me into a very awkward situation and you got me out of it. So, I would say that the one cancels the other, wouldn't you? How's life treating you?"

"Oh, so-so. Just started, but you know how it is. This war, it's changed things. People don't have any money."

"So true," said the Major and shook his head ruefully. "Hard to find decent card players these days. I'm on my way to the club for lunch. Why not shut up shop and let's have a little chat?"

And so they walked down Bond Street, into Piccadilly and then down St. James Street until they came to Black's, a club that required 36 members' approval on a membership application. Most clubs only required two.

Entering, Mr. Pettibone could not help gazing around at the wonders of the club, including the members who, in various states of decrepitude, were passing their last days resplendently displayed on sofas and chairs.

"Don't gawp, Pettibone. It's rude," and the Major steered Mr. Pettibone to the dining room.

"So, you're an art dealer now, Pettibone?" asked the major, and without waiting for a reply followed up with:

"I think that I might be able to put you in the way of some business if you would like. Of course, I should require a small commission, say 20 percent on any sales that might come from the introduction."

"Major! That sounds a little steep to me, said Mr. Pettibone, with a look of horror in his eyes, and a gleaming smile to match on his lips. Let's say 12.5 percent." And they settled at 15.

"That's done then," said the Major. "I do hate talking about money. If anyone overheard our conversation, I should be ejected from the club. Commerce is strictly forbidden on the premises. So let me tell you what's in the wind. An old school chum of mine is facing the problems that all of the upper classes are: colossal death duties (his father died last year and there is a vast estate), high taxes, and no liquidity. Unfortunately, he is forced to sell and the only things of value he feels are his furniture and paintings. Especially one picture. He doesn't want to sell, as most of the stuff has been in the family for generations, but ..."

"I understand, Major, and you would like me to make a valuation and either buy directly or sell the items on commission?"

"That's it. And I shall be grateful for that small cut that we have agreed on. Tell you what, I'll call up Jack from the lobby and we can arrange to go down to take a squint if you would like."

Within a very short time it was settled, and the following day the Major was parked outside Mr. Pettibone's shop in his ancient Rolls Royce, a monster of a thing with a mouse of an engine. Mr. Pettibone got in and sniffed. He couldn't help it: There was a distinct smell, a mixture of leather, wood (walnut, specifically), wax, petrol, cigar, and mildew — just like a good claret, had Mr. Pettibone been inclined towards oenophilia. Which he wasn't: A stout's the thing for me, he would say when asked what his 'poison' might be.

The drive to Staybrookshire was pleasant enough and the weather had taken upon itself to clear into one of those warmer, clammy days of late winter that are such a token of a maritime climate. They turned in at the lodge, vacant of course, and the gates gaped open, with the one on the left coming off its upper hinges, leaning forward despondently in the hope of an uplifting experience. At the door of the Tudor house (with Georgian additions), the Stokes family awaited their arrival. Mr. Stokes stood next to his wife, a large and somewhat intimidating woman, and their son, Timothy, a fair-headed lad of sixteen, who was at Dorchester School.

Brief introductions were made and then more lengthy ones as they entered the Hall. The lighting was entirely through large, mullioned windows, some graced by coats of arms of Stokes' long past. Mr. Pettibone looked around appraisingly. His five years in prison had been put to very good use. He read everything he could on antique furniture and paintings, and when the library had been used to its fullest extent, he had been granted the privilege of having additional volumes sent in.

In the large Hall, there were some really good Gainsboroughs and some very bad Romneys, a Turner or two, and was that a row of Canalettos? The furniture was good too, some nice Adams pieces out of place in the Tudor style of the house, but clearly taken there from the Georgian additions. Dust was everywhere; Mr. Pettibone sneezed.

After lunch, they sat in the kitchen around a large deal table.

"Really, the only warm place in the house," said Mr. Stokes. "And we can't afford servants, even if we could find them. So, it's up to us to keep this place in order."

"Fighting a losing battle," said Lady Elizabeth Stokes. "So glad you're getting rid of the old eyesore."

"My mother's not a sentimentalist," added Tim.

"And are you?" asked the Major.

"Yes, in a sort of way. I shall miss this place."

"I'm sure you will, but if Mr. Pettibone does his job, perhaps you won't have to. Some of the stuff you have here must get enough to pay off the death duties and square you with the authorities."

"But not enough to keep this dump up," said Lady Elizabeth. Mr. Stokes took off his glasses and wiped the lenses. He was a rather indistinct person as dusty as the furniture, looking more a part of the fixtures than an animate object. Mr. Pettibone gazed around him as they left the kitchen to go on a tour so that he could make an appraisal of the contents. Taking a black leather-bound notebook from his breast pocket, he started to evaluate. He really was not sure about the amount realizable; times were hard and no one really wanted this stuff anymore. Shame: however, he thought that he might be able to flog some of it in the States, where there was still money around and people liked authenticity from the old country. On reaching the first landing, Mr. Stokes stopped.

"Now, Mr. Pettibone, I really want you to take a good look at this. This is my most valued possession"

And Mr. Pettibone did. It seemed to be a genuine Geminiani, thirteenth century. Part of a triptych, he thought. Evidently so, and he could make out the marks still visible where it had been levered out of the setting. The depiction was delectable. The Virgin Mary painted with a rapt expression, staring upward in a mixture of grief and anticipation. Unlike Lady Elizabeth, Pettibone was a sentimentalist, and he couldn't help being entranced by what he saw.

"It's got a bit of a story behind it, doesn't it, Dad?" said Tim.

"Oh, don't bore these gentlemen with more of your tales, Jack," said Lady Elizabeth. "I'm sure that they have had enough of this dump and want to get back to London and central heating as soon as possible."

The Major was not sure, as all the windows of his small flat had been blown out in the last days of the war, and he was still having difficulty finding a glazier.

"Before you go, have a glass of something with me in the library," said Mr. Stokes; so he, the Major, Mr. Pettibone and Tim re-entered the room. Lady Elizabeth had disappeared.

"Well, sit down. That painting that you have in your hands was not in my family. I got it towards the end of the war. I was stationed in Germany and was the military governor of Section D in Berlin. You should have seen the devastation. Scarcely a building standing and the people destitute and picking around the ruins scavenging for anything they could find. No food, no water, no warmth, no cigarettes. I had no

53

pity for them really. I thought that they got what they deserved; and my driver, Sergeant Brown, was even angrier with them than I. Our job was to maintain order as best we could, but Brown took every possible opportunity to humiliate any German he came across. A stray bomb missing the George V docks obliterated the entire street where he lived, taking his wife and infant child with it. He never forgave the Germans. And I think that most of us were in a similar mood, after what we had seen in the war. Well, one night, while we were on patrol to enforce the curfew, we turned a corner and saw a struggle going on in a side street. It seemed that a woman was holding something in her hands and two men were trying to take it from her. One of them had picked up a brick from a pile from a bombed building and had hit her a glancing blow on the forehead. Stunned she had fallen to the floor.

'Stop the car, Brown,' I said.

'Why, Sir? Let them get on with it. They deserve to die, every last one of them.'

'Have you no decency, man?' I asked.

'None, Sir. Not when it comes to them.'

'Stop the car. That's an order.'

"And so he did and I got out. One of the men ran off and the other had the object that he had wrested from the woman under one arm and was about to drop a heavy boulder on her head with the other. I drew out my revolver and fired a shot just above his head. He dropped the boulder and the other object and ran off. As I approached, I noticed a rank smell and looking at the object saw that it was a dead cat, probably a few days old. The woman had found it and was going to make a stew, she told me, but she had come across these two in the road and they, in their hunger, had tried to take it from her. She slowly rose to her feet. Her English was excellent and she mentioned that she had been an English teacher before the war. Her husband had been a gauleiter for the district but had been shot while confronting some soldiers a few days earlier and her only son had been killed on the Eastern Front. Despondent, she had been combing the ruins like so many others for something to eat, more of a reflex than a desire to live. I supported her and wondered what to do next.

'Why didn't you let them kill me? It would have been a mercy,' she said.

'Common decency,' I replied. 'There has been too little of it in this war. Perhaps I'm trying to reclaim some. Come with me.'

"She was frightened. 'Are you going to arrest me?' she asked, and I am sure that she had visions of the light interrogatory methods that the Gestapo used on their hapless victims.

'No, I'm going to give you a meal.'

"When we reached the car, I could see an insubordinate frown on Brown's face. 'Open the door, Sergeant, and let us in.'

"He slowly and grudgingly got out of the car.

'Take us back to HQ,' I ordered. 'This woman is to be questioned.'

"And he drove on. When we reached the building, I got out and opened the door for her, and I could see the contempt on Brown's face. Contempt for me, as though I were a traitor; and perhaps I was, but all I could see was the hunger in this woman's face and the uncertain future facing her. I couldn't do anything about the latter, but I might be able to help her at least here and now. The sentries snapped smartly to attention and saluted. We went to a sitting-room, and I called for the orderly, who after attending to her head wound brought in my supper. When he had gone, I gave it to her and unquestioningly she grabbed the plate and gulped down the food.

'When have you last eaten a meal?' I asked.

'I have no idea,' she said. I called for the orderly and ordered another meal. He looked at me very oddly and said, 'Sorry, Sir. Rationing and all that. Only one supper, even for colonels.' And he looked at the woman, and then at me and there was a clear understanding in his features. "But I'll see what I can do.' And he came back a few minutes later with some bread and cheese. 'All I could find Sir,' which he put in front of the woman.

"After she left, my adjutant came to see me. Smartly saluting first, and then when told to be at ease, he informed me that Brown had asked to be transferred and did I mind. 'No,' I said wearily. 'Let him go.'

'I'll have someone else for you in the AM, Sir.'

"Next morning when I was about to leave the HQ, a corporal from the front desk ran up. "This was left for you, Sir. Better be careful opening it. Could be a bomb. You know what them Jerries is like. Sneaky like.'

"I took the paper parcel, unwrapped it and found the painting that you have there, and a note and photograph. The letter said:

Dear Sir (I am sorry but I never asked you for your name),

Thank you for your compassion, so very rare in these times. I have nothing to give you in return except this picture that was in my family. I thought the expression on the Madonna's face so sad, and yet so beautiful. I hope you will take it, and perhaps think that despite everything there is goodness to be found. I have found goodness in you. There is also a photograph in my house with the picture, and a newspaper with a date on the desk in front of it establishing that this was in our possession long before Hitler, so that you can see it is not loot.

God protect you, as He will not me. Like all Germans, I share in collective damnation for what we have done.

Ilse Muller

"And so, gentlemen, I got this picture. I asked the authorities whether I could take it back with me, and after a little research they agreed that it was not loot. And now, I must sell it. And like Ilse Muller, I will be losing my home, too. There won't be much left for you either, Tim, old man. I am sorry."

"That's alright, Dad," said Tim. But from the boy's expression, Mr. Pettibone saw that it clearly wasn't.

Mr. Pettibone had been turning the painting over in his hands and then took it to the window so that he could see things a little more clearly. From his pocket he removed a glass and put that in his eye, while the Major slowly stuffed his pipe with tobacco.

"You know, Mr. Stokes, this really is a most remarkable painting. From what I have seen today, I would say that I could get a good sum from the sale of your other things. Especially the Canalettos. I could get you an excellent price for everything in America if you will let me. But I would hang on to this picture. For one thing, there is not much of a market for paintings of this type these days. Too religious, too sentimental, and the times are out of sorts to appreciate this. Hang on to it, Sir. It has so much meaning for you. A reminder of the kindness that there is in us, perhaps?"

On the way back to London, the Major asked Mr. Pettibone why he had done what he did. Surely every bit helped even if the Geminiani only got a small sum. The Stokes' were not in a position to be denied even the smallest help.

"True, true, Major," said Mr. Pettibone.

"Then why, man, did you do it?"

"Well, I hadn't the heart."

"What?" exclaimed the Major.

"The painting's clearly a fake. Didn't want to spoil it for him. And I think that the meaning of the painting is much more important than its value, don't you?"

The Major did not answer and put his foot on the accelerator.

Chapter 2: The Fall of Mann

It was cold at the aerodrome. Not for the first time that early morning Mr. Pettibone had run off to chase after his hat as it rolled crown over brim down the tarmac. "Streuth," he said as he blew into his hands and stamped his feet. It was nice of Mr. Mann to offer him a seat on his private plane. They both needed to go to Paris that day; Mr. Pettibone to attend a fine art auction and Mr. Mann for financial reasons. Mr. Pettibone knew little of the world of finance, but despite his ignorance, what he did know was Mr. Mann.

He had appeared on the scene comparatively recently and had captivated London and the headlines with his lavish lifestyle and parties to match. Entertaining carpenters and kings, but who knew where the money really came from? But who cared? He was solid enough as anyone could see, and his private bank, Mann et Cie, was obviously a considerable concern. His client list grew and included the rich, not so rich, those who wanted to be thought of as rich but weren't, and anyone who was anyone associated with the stage.

Mr. Mann had come into Mr. Pettibone's small shop looking for a particular painting and had found it there. Unlike his usual clients, Mr. Mann did not haggle over the price; he gave him the delivery address in St. James Square and started a casual conversation. They then went off to have dinner at Mr. Mann's place, and Mr. Pettibone had once again felt himself somewhat ill at ease. He couldn't explain why. Yes, of course the surroundings were lavish; yes, the servants were smooth, anticipated every wish and were exemplary; and yes, Mr.

Pettibone's cockney accent was out of place here. But there was something else; an indefinable something else that Mr. Pettibone could not quite put his finger on. And he left it at that.

Pettibone waited for Mr. Mann. It seemed like the whole world was waiting for Mr. Mann. A man in uniform approached. The pilot. "Have you seen Mr. Mann?" he asked. Mr. Pettibone looked at his shoes and then at the pilot. "No," he said. Perhaps Mr. Mann had forgotten; perhaps he had decided to take the train. Perhaps … Mr. Pettibone's spirits rose. He had never flown for two very good reasons: the first, that he could not afford to do it; the second that he was terrified. Those things weren't reliable, anyone could tell you that. Why, oh why had he agreed? But Mr. Mann had charm and also an excellent stock of booze, and in a befuddlement of excellent scotch and bonhomie, Mr. Pettibone had consented to join him on this trip and also to let him have a small part of Pettibone, Sons and Langford, Dealers and Valuers of Fine Antiques, for a consideration. That consideration was to be the handling of all of Mr. Pettibone's investments. Mr. Mann had questioned Mr. Pettibone for a long time about his financial position (which to tell the truth was not great), but had apparently also condescended to control the financial management of his business, waiving all fees in return.

"First class," said Mr. Pettibone, "absolutely first class," and Mr. Mann had looked at him a little strangely and took another large draft of his water. Mr. Mann did not drink.

More foot stamping in the cold in the early morning, and Mr. Pettibone turned towards the hut with the intention of ordering a taxi and going back to town. Once inside the hut, he heard a tremendous cacophony, and turning round saw a three-motored airplane taxiing out from a hanger. It was a Ford Trimotor and looked none too safe. As the plane drew closer, the wings appeared to shake. Mr. Pettibone was continuing with his arrangements to get back to town, when suddenly a hand clapped him on the shoulder and turning 'round he saw Mr. Mann.

"So sorry to be late, Mr. Pettibone. Please forgive me. But the Duke of Kent …"

Mr. Pettibone forgave him, and with somewhat grudging steps accompanied Mr. Mann out onto the tarmac.

59

"You know, Mr. Pettibone," said Mr. Mann with a slight accent, possibly French, thought Mr. Pettibone, but he could not be sure, "I really enjoy flying; it's that sense of being above everything. The world looks so beautiful from that great height. You could think that you owned the whole world. Of course, I haven't always been in this position you know …"

He was clearly going on with a tale of his past, but the sound of the engines swallowed the words as the plane came to a rest outside the hut, like an obedient pet waiting to be stroked lovingly by its master. Mr. Mann leapt up the steps to the aeroplane; he was agile, and he was short. Dyed red hair, under a homburg hat and his ill-fitting coat tails flapping behind him, as the breeze brewed up and caught them. Mr. Pettibone somewhat reluctantly followed.

On board there were two mahogany-paneled compartments separated by a door. The forward one was for Mr. Mann and had seats for three others. In front of that was the pilot's compartment. Aft of the main cabin was another compartment with space for two, already occupied by a stenographer and Mr. Mann's personal secretary, the former and for that matter the latter both being very young and very personable. Mr. Pettibone smiled wryly to himself and wondered …

"Charles, give Mr. Pettibone a drink, he looks as though he needs it."

"A little too early for me, Sir," replied Mr. Pettibone.

"Nonsense, you look terrible. Afraid of flying, are you?"

"Er …" replied Mr. Pettibone and then gratefully swallowed in one gulp the full beaker of scotch given him by Charles, the secretary.

Behind the aft compartment was another door that separated what was a vestibule from the rest of the airplane. It contained a cupboard for luggage, now filled completely, and a door to the left, which was for the lavatory. The door facing it was that providing access to the fuselage.

Looking at Charles as he took a draft from the second full beaker of scotch he was offered to steady his nerves, Mr. Pettibone noted a passing resemblance between the two, him and Mr. Mann. Shrewdly, Mr. Mann caught Mr. Pettibone's expression and laughed.

"No, we are not related. You like to think so, Charles, don't you?"

Charles shrugged his shoulders and looked away, but not before Mr. Pettibone detected a dejected and perhaps malicious expression. "That one's trouble," he thought to himself.

"No, Charles' father was a good friend of mine, as was his wife, and when Charles' father died, I wanted to do something for the lad."

"Thanks for nothing," said Charles in a half voice.

"What was that, Charles?" asked Mr. Mann.

"Nothing."

Later, as he handed Mr. Pettibone his third drink in the aft compartment, Charles whispered, "Don't be fooled by that old shit. He ruined my father, and he will probably ruin you."

"Don't be absurd," said Pettibone for no other reason than that by now he was more than a little tipsy, and he wobbled unsteadily, aided by the stenographer, back to his seat in the forward compartment next to Mr. Mann.

"Shall you be needing me on this trip, Sir?" she asked.

Mr. Mann thought very carefully it appeared, and somewhat reluctantly said, "No, Dorothy, not today. I shall be returning this evening. Mrs. Mann will be out, and I shall be in need of someone to help me host a small dinner party this evening. Would you be available?"

"Of course, Mr. Mann." And as she turned her back, Mr. Pettibone noticed that Mr. Mann's gaze was appraisingly aimed at her backside and hips. He wished he hadn't drunk so much now. He was clearly imagining things, but sometimes two and two did make four.

Charles returned and asked whether there was anything else required from him before they landed at Le Bourget.

Mr. Mann looked at him somewhat tenderly. "No, thank you, Charles," and as Charles turned towards the aft compartment, Mr. Pettibone noticed that Mr. Mann gazed at Charles' backside and hips. He again wished that he had not drunk so much, but if two and two did not make four, sometimes it made three.

He settled back in his seat as the engines revved up.

In the air, Mr. Mann was shuffling papers and looked increasingly disgruntled.

"Humph," he said finally and threw them disgustedly onto the floor.

"You know, Mr. Mann, that I have absolutely no head for finance," said Mr. Pettibone.

"I gathered that," was the mordant reply. "You haven't missed anything."

"Except wealth," was the response.

"There is that of course, and also the ulcers."

"Well, you must be very smart to have achieved all of this," said Mr. Pettibone wistfully.

"Very smart and perhaps a little, shall we say, oblique? Not unlike you Pettibone."

"What's that supposed to mean?"

"Well, certainly ability is necessary in my field, but also perhaps an off-centre approach. Just as in your life you were an excellent forger of five-pound notes. An artist in your own way, but shall we call your métier an off-centre approach?"

"Oh ... how did you know of that?" asked Mr. Pettibone.

"A little bird told me," said Mr. Mann, and he raised his right index finger placing it gently against his right nostril.

"That's all over with," said Mr. Pettibone and flushed. "My conscience is clear."

"Well now, is it? Is it really? I don't think people ever go straight once they veer from the path of legality," said Mr. Mann cynically. "I don't believe such people have a conscience at all. Or if they do, it doesn't last long. And has no effect. Otherwise, they wouldn't commit a crime in the first place. Being a crook takes a lot of effort. Wouldn't a conscience put a block on all that? A real conscience I mean. No, you don't have a conscience, a real conscience any more than I."

"Are you a crook then?" asked Mr. Pettibone, a little anxious. He remembered the agreement he had made regarding the management of his business and investments.

"What a sad thought. I have mingled with many; in fact, some very big ones are my best friends. But then you have to mix with everyone these days," he said, "even you." And he gave a loud laugh.

Charles came into the compartment and immediately the atmosphere changed. It was tense and Mr. Mann had lost his composure. In response to a comment that Mr. Pettibone could not hear, he got out of his seat and slapped Charles' face. How very odd, thought Mr. Pettibone. Generally, it's women who slap men, and fathers their sons, not man to man. A punch would be more like it. Now I wonder … And looking at the two, Mr. Pettibone was again struck by the resemblance that Charles had to his boss. But if so, why did Mr. Mann appear to be interested in other more basic attributes that hinted at something a little less than paternal? He let that one go, a thought that was most likely driven by the intoxicants he had imbibed.

"Mr. Pettibone needs another scotch," ordered Mr. Mann, "and be quick about it, lad."

Charles stomped off fuming and on bringing back the unneeded drink whispered to Mr. Pettibone as he served him, "That man likes to hurt people. Someone will kill him if he doesn't do himself in first."

"What?" asked Mr. Pettibone.

"Do you know what an Achilles' heel is?" asked Charles.

"Yes," said Mr. Pettibone hesitatingly.

"Well, his is that he has a conscience. Odd that for a sharp businessman. It's a strange conscience, and warped, but he has one. And it will be the death of him. I'm his conscience."

"Charles, get out. Now! You have work to do, and so do I."

"Now Mr. Pettibone, you were telling me that crooks have real consciences?"

"Was I?"

"Well, you must have been because you were arguing with me when I said, once a crook always a crook. Surely if you have a conscience, that would stop you, wouldn't it?"

"I don't know," said Mr. Pettibone, and he continued, "When I was a lad, perhaps about 15, I did something very stupid."

"We all do," said Mr. Mann.

"No, this was … um, well. So my aunt and uncle down the road from where my Ma and Pa lived owned a small tobacconist shop. Sweets, cigarettes, newspapers, and the occasional under-the-counter contraceptive; you know, that sort of thing."

Mr. Mann nodded.

"Well, one Saturday my uncle came over and asked whether I could mind the shop as he and his missus were going up to town to do some shopping. There would be my small cousin, Kat — that's Cathleen — their daughter who was 6 at the time, and I would have to look after her and give her supper, but she was no trouble. She was a good kid. I was a little miffed as I wanted to watch the local club, which was playing football in the park by the gasworks, but my dad said, 'Of course he will. You don't mind, Bert, do you?'

"And off I went. It was a slow afternoon, and not many customers. The till had always intrigued me, even from when I was very small, and so I decided I would play with it. Pressing the keys and hearing the bell as I closed the drawer. As I did this after a while, I noticed that there was money in the till. Of course there was, but it was quite a large amount. You see it was Saturday and the till was usually emptied of the week's takings on Saturday night. The shop was closed on Sundays. As I played with the till, I was less mesmerized by the bell as by the cash. I thought that if I took a small amount, they wouldn't miss it. There was so much in there. That's what a child would think, and that's what I thought. So on the next go-round, I quickly put my hand in, took out a few notes without looking, and pushed the drawer closed with a loud thud. I closed my eyes and took a quick breath. On opening them, I saw Kat looking at me. She had a strange expression, and I knew that she knew. She said nothing and turned to go out of the room.

'It's time for your supper,' I said, and there was a quiver in my voice.

"She said nothing, and she looked at her plate when I gave it to her. 'Bubble and squeak,' I said; 'smashing.' No response from her.

"A little later her parents returned.

'Hello, Bert. Kat kept you busy? I'll be with you in a minute,' said my uncle as he stood in the hall hanging his coat on the hat stand and taking off his scarf. 'Gert,' he said to his wife, 'hold my tea for a bit. I'm just going to take out the till.'

"I was aware of a panic that rose suddenly and kicked me in the stomach.

'You all right, Bert?'

'Yes, Auntie.'

'Well, you'd better be off home then. Thanks for minding the place and for looking after Kat.'

'She was no trouble, no trouble at all Auntie. Bye!' And I rushed out of the house.

"That evening we had a surprise visit from Uncle Fred.

'Darnedest thing,' he said. 'The takings were a few pounds less than they should be.'

'How do you know?' my father asked glancing up from the paper.

'I counted 67 pounds Friday, so there should've been more than that today. But there were only 65 in the till. And you know what?'

'No, surprise me.'

'That little minx Kat says she done it. She came up to me while I was counting and she said she done it. I asked her why and she said she dunno. She just done it, and then burnt the notes in the grate. Why you done that? I asked. Dunno, she said. Well, I beat her and so did her Ma, and there was no food for her that night, I can tell you.'

'Isn't that a bit hard; she's only 6."

'She wouldn't answer why and was a little obstinate miss, crossed her arms and pursed her lips like. Well, Ma and I showed her.'

"I was speechless. I wanted to say something, but all that came out was a croak. I could feel the notes in my pocket. It was as though they were on fire.

'Bert, did you know anything about this?' asked Uncle Fred.

'No,' I managed to say. I wanted to say I done it. I really did. I couldn't.

'Uncle Fred …'

'Yes, Bert?'

'Nuffink.'

"And I left it at that. Shortly after I went out and threw the money in the canal. I could never understand why Kat didn't spill the beans about me."

"Hero worship?" suggested Mr. Mann sarcastically.

"Who knows?"

"So, you had a conscience, did you? But didn't own up," Mr. Mann guffawed.

"No."

"I don't believe you for a moment. You couldn't face the consequences. That was reason, and reason overcame your conscience. That is if you really had one in the first place. Which I doubt. You threw the money away because you didn't want to be caught. Destroy the evidence!"

Mr. Pettibone looked crestfallen.

"And this supposed conscience of yours never made you do anything crooked for the rest of your life?" Mr. Mann snorted and fixed Mr. Pettibone with a stern look. "Rather proves my point, doesn't it?" he asked.

Mr. Pettibone was deflated.

"Anyway, I have to go to the lavatory," said Mr. Mann.

And so saying, he opened the door to the aft cabin. Charles came in to join Mr. Pettibone shortly after.

"His Nibs said he'd rather sit alone for a moment. What did you say to him?"

"About what?"

"I don't know … anything. He looked a little shaken, and I thought he might be thinking something over."

"That Antilles thing?"

"Achilles, yes. Perhaps."

"I don't think people like him have consciences," said Mr. Pettibone, "despite what you said."

A short while later the plane landed at Le Bourget. Mr. Mann was not with them.

"I thought he was in the back cabin," said Mr. Pettibone, perturbed.

"So did I," said Charles, "and that's where I left him."

The police came, took statements and went. The coastguard was alerted, but the pilot could give no information to help them. The papers had a field day:

Missing Magnate: Mann's empire unmanned. Fraudulent activity. Where's the cash?

Apparently, things had not been quite so much on the up and up that Mr. Mann would have liked his clients to believe.

Charles came to the George V Hotel where Mr. Pettibone was staying.

"Successful auction, Sir?"

"Yes, very."

"Shame about Mr. Mann, isn't it?" And Charles looked intently at Mr. Pettibone. "He must have gone out of the wrong door by accident, or perhaps he jumped?"

"Or perhaps he was pushed," said Mr. Pettibone, and putting his glass of beer down on the bar counter, gave Charles a very straight stare and walked out.

Chapter 3: The End of the Line

The spring of 1942 was not Britain's finest hour. There had been several defeats and the loss of some capital ships. The country plunged into a certain gloom. The bombing of London continued unabated and the suffering experienced could not be adequately described. But for Mr. Pettibone, 1942 was an excellent year: He had just been released from prison and embracing a newfound enthusiasm he was off to do his bit for his country. A private soldier manning an anti-aircraft battery on the south coast. The Major was also experiencing a change: He had recently re-married for the fourth time, or was it the fifth?

He knew that he always said this with each of his former matrimonial adventures, but this really was different. Until now, he felt he had not known what love was really like. Lust yes, the occasional sentimental twinge, yes. But gut-blinding, total committing, unrelenting love, no. No, for him this was as though an explosion had gone off in his soul and shattered forever his perspective of life.

He came down to breakfast feeling completely content, and since his marriage a year or so ago (coming up to his anniversary, shouldn't he do something to celebrate?) he felt the world was a wonderful place. Gone was his cynicism; she had swept that aside. And love, he pondered as he came down the stairs, well it was a new experience for him to feel that complete and holy rapture of unquestioning and unquestioned delight. Even the English Breakfast tea was refreshing. He had hated English Breakfast tea: There was nothing

English about it, and why should it be solely for breakfast he wondered. Why is there no Scottish dinner tea? Well, for a very good reason he supposed: Tea was rarely taken after dinner and the English were associated with tea, so someone somewhere had the idea to market a new blend under that nomenclature. But Mary liked it, and for him, that was all that counted.

He glanced through the breakfast things to where his wife was bending over the paper and marveled at how she could possibly have seen anything in him. Lady Cylburn, as she became (he had been able to drop the Buller by Royal Decree) was clearly as happy as he was. Serene, content. Of course, her money was certainly one thing. No more did he need to earn a living in the card rooms of the clubs in St. James. No, she gave him a respectable life. He pondered what it was exactly that he gave her. Certainly, a title, but these were two-a-penny for a person like her. Besides, she was no snob. But what was it that she saw? Perhaps she thought he was someone worth saving. He couldn't agree that he was worth the effort, but the fact that she saw something, each day put a spring in his step.

"John," she said looking up from her kedgeree.

"Yes?"

"You're going into town today?"

"Yes. I need to go to Trumpets for a hair trimming and I thought that I might go to the club for lunch."

She frowned.

"No, there will be no cards. I've finished with that."

And he knew that the depth of their intimacy brooked no lies. She did, too, and that understanding meant that no further discussion on this point was necessary.

"John, Margery rang me up."

"Yes?" he asked again. There was a coolness in his response. Margery, Mary's sister, he felt, did not quite see him the same way his wife did. He was certain she disapproved of the marriage, and he could see that, from her point of view, she was right. He had little to offer: a patchy war record in the last war, and a brilliant mind given to earning a living by playing cards —well, not exactly a recommendation for anyone who was aspiring to marriage with Mary, her youngest sister.

"She wondered whether you would take Nicholas to lunch."

Nicholas was his nephew by marriage. He was now in his final year at Dorchester, and would be called up, it was sure.

"Oh?"

"Well, he is rather at a difficult stage. Final term and all of that. And it wouldn't matter so much, but he is probably going into the Navy as soon as term ends."

John looked serious.

"The Navy?"

"He loves ships and is desperate. Margery thinks he has already been given a junior commission but can't get him to tell her. She is at her wit's end with worry."

"He's in the OTC and that would naturally have meant an Army commission. I wonder what strings he pulled for the Navy."

"All Margery can see is a sinking ship, and ratings in the sea burning to death in a cauldron of boiling oil. Like his father, you know. He was in the Navy. She is terrified."

"I can understand that."

"She wonders whether you might have a word with him, and with your experience guide him?"

"Guide him?"

"Well, perhaps a job at the ministry here in London? He speaks several languages fluently, and I think he's quite bright. He has been given a scholarship at Cardinal College, Oxford but they will defer it for the duration."

"At the ministry? I don't know."

"Well, you know people at the ministry …?"

"Well, yes, but pulling strings and all that. I don't know. Besides, he will probably be safer in the Navy than anywhere else."

"But what about Intelligence?"

"Couldn't say really."

John tugged at the sleeves of his own uniform. He had been in the first war and recommissioned into the second as an acting colonel. He was surprised, because although his courage was not in question, his moral failings had been. And his medals were initially denied on the grounds that he had been involved in a little misunderstanding with the mess accounts. Nonetheless, he showed "conspicuous gallantry" and had been demobbed as a major and the other issues set aside. He was now in uniform again and joined his old regiment, the Staybrookshire Regiment (known as the Stanx), but without the foggiest notion yet of what he was supposed to do.

"You know, Mary, I will gladly do my best, but I am not sure I have any influence whatsoever."

"Well, try to talk him out of the Navy, for God's sake."

"Yes, of course my dear. I will do anything I can."

And while his wife went out to telephone her sister and set things up, he looked morosely out of the window. 'This war was a real bugger,' he thought. 'More sacrifice and more young lives wasted. Another generation lost.'

Emerging from Green Park underground station, he walked slowly down St. James Street towards Pall Mall. Margery had set it up that Nicholas would meet him by the steps of John's club in a small square in that neighborhood.

John didn't know what to say. He was not good at this sort of thing. In fact, the idea that he had any advice to give seemed strange-strange and not a little uncomfortable. He always went through life reacting rather than analyzing. At heart he felt he maintained the outlook and maturity of a 15-year-old schoolboy. He shook his head. Two smart, young officers saluted as he came to the end of the street, and he returned their salutation.

Gloomily and not a little nervously, he turned into the square. Sandbags had been put around the buildings as around the others he had passed. Some of them also had sentries on duty, as dignitaries were known to lunch in the London clubs. A shadow suddenly crept over him as he walked with head bowed, and looking up he saw the ungainly, bloated bulk of a barrage balloon as it drifted above him, aimlessly in the wind.

Reaching his club, he climbed the steps and opened the door. The drabness of the interior had not really struck him before. But this was the first time he had been there since his marriage. His perspective had changed. He thought that the exclusiveness of London clubs was directly proportional to their shabbiness.

"Hello, Uncle John?"

A cheerful voice greeted him, and a boy got up from a seat by the porter's desk and bounded forward enthusiastically.

"Oh, hello Nick," said John Cylburn, acting colonel, and shook the hand proffered. He noticed a slight flinch.

"Don't like being called Nick?"

"Don't mind, Sir."

"But you do. What do they call you at school?"

"My friends call me. ... Well ..." And the boy was clearly embarrassed.

"Well, I shall call you Nicholas. Would that be alright?"

"Yes, Sir."

"Good. Then let's have a drink." And Colonel Sir John Cylburn felt he would need it. He steered the boy into the American bar.

"Hello, Sir John," said the barman. "Haven't seen you for a long time."

"No. I would like a nice MacAllen if you have one."

"Yes, Sir. Ten, twelve or fifteen?"

"Oh, ten. There's a war on you know. I can't afford the others." The barman laughed. "What'll you have Nicholas?" asked John.

"A pint of Bass, Uncle John."

The barman frowned. "How old is he, Sir?"

"Oh, I can vouch for him."

"Yes, I know, but the rules are ..."

"I know the rules. But he's 18, (John lied), and about to go into the ... services and well, I think ...you know what I mean."

And the barman pulled a pint of Bass and slid it over to Nicholas.

"Thanks awfully," he said.

"I'm sure that this isn't your first. And from what I know about Dorchester, you could probably knock back several of those and be as sober as a judge. Or at least appear to be. Are judges always sober by the way, do you think, Nicholas?"

"Don't know, Sir," said his nephew.

"Now your mother is concerned about something" he said after a pause. "And I won't conceal it from you that she and your aunt have asked me to talk to you about it."

"Yes?"

"Do you really want to join the Navy?"

"Yes, awfully."

"Why?"

"I want to die at sea"

"What?" asked John.

"I want to die at sea," Nicholas repeated.

"No one wants you to die," said John stunned.

"I am going to die in this war, and so I want to die at sea. I don't know why, but there's a comfort in it for me."

"I don't think you know what you're talking about," said John, nonplussed. "Have you ever seen men die? Do you have any idea what it is like? How can you be so stupid?"

Nicholas looked upset but not ashamed.

"I'm not a coward and I want to fight. And I just know that I won't make it."

"That's the most defeatist and stupid comment I've ever heard." And John was now completely perplexed."

"I know, because … because I've been told."

"For God's sake? For God's sake," and John looked at the boy in disbelief. His features were earnest. The dark bangs framed the side of his unfurrowed forehead; his thin face had a facile beauty that only innocence brings.

"Sir, God told me."

The boy clearly believed it. Could he be mad? thought John. He was completely out of his depth.

"You're delusional," was all that John could say. What could possibly have happened?

"I just have a repeated dream of lying surrounded by water, looking up at the sky and being at peace. I want to die that way."

"And you think that's a message?"

"Yes."

"A message from God?"

"Yes. I believe so."

"And the pain?"

"Oh, there's no pain. I can't feel a thing. Just gratitude that I have done my bit."

"You're completely insane. But look, I don't want to upset your digestion. The food here is still the best in London. We'll come back to that in a sec."

"On another note, there is something that has been worrying me," said John, "and I would like to have your thoughts, Nicholas."

"As you know I have no heir and well, I don't think it likely that your aunt and I will have any children."

Nicholas shuffled in his seat.

"So, I was wondering how you might feel if I could get the ball rolling to designate you as the heir to the baronetcy. You are an only child, and I have no direct relations. I will have to get advice from the College of Heralds, and possibly even a dispensation from the palace because of the absence of a direct bloodline. What do you think?"

"Well, of course I should like that, Uncle. I should like that very much."

"I'm not sure that it will work, but I will certainly do my best. It's an old title you know and I would hate to see it vanish."

"Yes, Sir, but ..."

"Oh, that. That's only a dream. Dreams have a surprising ability to be forgotten. And they never come true. Besides, I am going to get you a commission in my regiment. That will be easy and now don't argue, it's done."

Nicholas was about to reply but clearly changed his mind. And they went into the dining room.

As the trolley was being drawn up by the waiter and he raised the lid to uncover the beef Wellington, a shadow crept over the table.

"Never thought to see you here, Cylburn," said a voice. Cultured, but menacing at the same time.

"Hello, Staybrook, how are you?"

"Ruined and you know it. Who's the lad?"

"Staybrook, my nephew, Nicholas Farnham. Nicholas, Lord Staybrook. Won't you join us?" asked John, hoping desperately that he wouldn't.

"I wouldn't eat with you if it were the only meal I was ever going to have. Do you know what your uncle did to me, young man?"

Nicholas was colouring and looking decidedly ill-at-ease.

"He destroyed me, that's what he did. He cheats at cards and ruins people. Why someone hasn't killed him by now is a mystery, why I've half a mind ..."

And he lurched forward but was prevented from falling onto the table by two waiters who led him away.

Nicholas looked shocked.

"I don't know whether your mother told you about me. I, well, I didn't have the luck or the backbone I should have had. I made a living playing cards with people. I generally won. I had a gift. Could remember the cards. I have an excellent memory and also I can work things out in my head. That's how I survived until I met your aunt. She changed my life. Never played a game since we married. Never will again. I'm ashamed of my past, but I did not cheat."

"But, Uncle. That man. Gosh. He was so angry."

"Well, so would I be if I had lost all my money. I'm sorry about it now. But I wasn't then. It was survival."

"Rather like war," said Nicholas.

"Well, you're going to have to survive this one. I need you take the title and pass it on. Did you see his moustache by the way?" asked John, changing the subject. "Didn't it look just like …"

And they both laughed.

It was getting dark when they left the club. On the steps, John turned to his nephew.

"Now, have you given any more thought to this Navy business? I am going to get you a commission in the Army whether you like it or not."

Nicholas looked at his uncle. He said nothing.

It had been raining for some time and the road in the square was wet and glistening. Here and there, there were puddles of water. One of these was deep and fairly wide, a crater where heavy vehicles had dug a large hole in the soft tarmac. They were walking across the road when a car drove towards them. John thought little of it, but it quickly accelerated. It was making towards him.

Suddenly he was pushed, and he thought to himself, 'Damn, so that's how it's all going to end. In a car accident? How ironic.' And he heard an impact, then a dull thud, and then what sounded like a resigned sigh. But none of this came from him. He looked 'round. People were running towards the crater. A figure lay in the water. The shock wore off and John looked down at his nephew and saw the life slowly draining from his eyes. There was a peaceful smile on his lips as he looked at his uncle. And then he died.

The man in the car stroked his small, black moustache in agitation. Looking in the rearview mirror, he shouted, "Damn!"

A dense crushing fell on John, which he knew was not physical. He wanted to shout; he wanted to cry; he wanted … But he could not. As the people gathered around the corpse lying in that pool of water, he gave way to an inward grief so powerful that there was no emotion no physical expression that could contain it.

"Poor bugger," an onlooker mumbled. But before anything else could be said or done, the mournful wail of the air-raid siren tortured the air. The crowd of people, as one, surged towards the air raid shelter in the middle of the square, bearing John in their midst as the anti-aircraft guns started up and the searchlights rent the pitch-black sky.

Chapter 4: Triptych

The Reverend Riordan Nash was enthusiastic about his calling, despite (or perhaps, because of) his patrician background. He had felt it appropriate to expiate that sin by joining the church. His ministry was selected by the Bishop and was as a prison chaplain to one of the larger, and less salubrious, institutions of incarceration. While there, his life experience was broadened by association with such interesting people as child molesters, murderers and the occasional necrophiliac.

All of this, while initially disturbing, led him to understand that even such people have lives outside their chosen vocation, and could be interesting — and conversationalists, intelligent and pleasant to be with. But he fortunately had his faith to sustain him, and this precluded any possibility of temptation, however hard his newly found friends in that cloistered environment may have tried to entice him.

Mr. Pettibone had looked at the letter he received from the Rev. Mr. Nash with a certain degree of skepticism. For one thing, he did not like the country and so was reluctant to take up any invitation to that region which occupies the major part of England. In addition, he did not believe in revisiting the past. All of that had been put behind him, and he was justifiably proud of what he had accomplished as a dealer in fine art, albeit in a small way. So it was despite his better judgment that he found himself outside the small railway station at Chelmsborough in the county of Staybrookshire, abbreviated for the benefit of the Post Office as Stanx. He had not long to wait before an ancient and battered

Ford motorcar drew up, and springing from the driver seat sprung the Rev. Mr. Nash, with hair waving in the breeze.

"Albert, I am so very pleased to see you," said the Rev. Mr. Nash in his very enthusiastic manner. His earnestness was reinforced by the fact that he was 29 years old and still saw the world as his to conquer and to put to rights. Mr. Pettibone had seen a good deal more of the world and his enthusiasm was suitably tempered by experience.

"So nice to see you," he replied. "Absolutely first class." He climbed into the seat next to the Rev. Mr. Nash. The journey to the old rectory was one of extraordinary chaos. The Rev. Mr. Nash, while no doubt being a man of God, was not a man of the road. Such traffic lights as there were, were ignored, pedestrians remained unseen and took their own lives in their hands when he passed. As for wildlife, well the least said about that the better.

On reaching the old rectory, the vicar sprang out and, before Mr. Pettibone could even attempt to, he had taken up his leather Gladstone bag and was manfully steering this towards the front door of what was clearly a Victorian attempt to recreate the glory days of the high Gothic. This attempt was not entirely successful. Mr. Pettibone however, despite his knowledge of the visual arts was not in the slightest bit interested in architecture, and the excesses of the style were allowed to pass without comment.

The housekeeper, a Mrs. Groynes, took the measure of Mr. Pettibone as she took his coat, and decided that here was another one, and one to be held at arm's length like all the others. The Rev. Mr. Nash, in a spasm of feeling, sparked by a sermon he had heard earlier that year by the Bishop of London, had come to the realization that the Church did not only need to support the soul, but had an immediate, more temporal role as well. So that being the case, he took pleasure in inviting those inmates of the prison system whose acquaintance he had made and who were deemed duly reformed, to come and stay with him, so that he could learn how he might be able to serve them better. Mr. Pettibone had been one such individual released during the war and who followed an exemplary path, putting his valuable experience as a forger of banknotes, and a very good one at that, to the service of art, especially that of the fifteenth century or earlier.

"You know, Vicar," said Mr. Pettibone, "It's a great shame that you no longer are at the Scrubs."

The Rev. Mr. Nash agreed but said that it was the Bishop's wish that he should take up this more rural post where he was needed.

It was difficult these days to find clergy who would be successful in such a community, and the Bishop had great confidence in the Rev. Mr. Nash's ability. He also felt that the prison environment might not be the best for such a tender mind as his. Besides, the Bishop, a very worldly individual despite his calling, thought that a less energetic and a more skeptical approach was needed in that position of prison chaplain.

"What will you have to drink?" asked the young Mr. Nash.

"A glass of stout would be capital," said Mr. Pettibone.

"Tea, coffee, or cocoa?"

"Come again?" asked Mr. Pettibone.

"We do not have alcohol in this house, I am afraid," the vicar said without a trace of sententiousness.

"First class," said Mr. Pettibone gloomily and then, "Cocoa."

They settled in the study, and after a few pleasantries, fell into a complete silence, which was broken about 10 minutes later by the sound of nailed shoes clomping their way down the uncarpeted stairs.

"Oh," said the vicar. "I may have forgotten to tell you that we have another graduate of the Scrubs with us. John Palindrome. Perhaps you know him?"

Mr. Pettibone shook his head.

"Ah, indeed, your paths probably did not cross. He would have been in a different wing of the Scrubs."

"Is that so?" commented Mr. Pettibone, whose interest in the weekend was fading fast.

"And what was he in for?"

"Oh, er ... Murder, I believe."

"You believe?" And Mr. Pettibone's voice had become shrill and rather concerned. "And you have him here in this house? And why wasn't he executed I want to know. Murder is a capital offense."

"Shush," said the vicar. "He's coming now. There was some allowance made for the circumstances of the crime, and the judge took the view that he would be able to benefit from rehabilitation. Also, his faith was important and that he is a Cambridge graduate. A plea for clemency was entered by the jury and approved by the Home Secretary."

Mr. Pettibone snorted into his handkerchief as the object of the discussion entered the room.

"John, I don't believe you know Mr. Pettibone," said the vicar, followed up by "Albert, this is Mr. Palindrome."

A quick glance told Mr. Pettibone all that he needed to know. A feeling of intense dislike overcame him, not for the crime but for Palindrome's appearance and manner. He was clearly effeminate, and his mincing ways were at odds with Mr. Pettibone's view of the order of the world. The artificial diction and the overzealous cut of his clothes added to Mr. Pettibone's disgust.

"How long were you in for?" he asked.

"Mr. Pettibone!" Exclaimed the vicar. "We don't ask such questions here. Once discharged, debts to society have been paid, and we are back in the world as equals."

"I wonder," muttered Mr. Pettibone.

"Mr. Pettibum, I hear that you were an excellent producer of banknotes," said Palindrome.

"Now, John, what did I just say?" said the vicar. "All of that is behind us."

Palindrome looked at Mr. Pettibone appraisingly.

"Did I see you at Covent Garden the other night? A spectacular Parsifal I thought."

"No," said Mr. Pettibone, clearly aware of where this was going.

"Perhaps we have met at the Strangeways club?"

Mr. Pettibone shuddered. Though few in the world of suburban niceties would know of the club, Mr. Pettibone's experience was wider. He would not have been seen dead in such a place, one in which assignations of the most dubious sort were made.

"No, definitely not," said Mr. Pettibone.

John Palindrome laughed. The laugh was not pleasant.

"So, Vicar, do you believe in guilt by association?" asked Palindrome.

"What?"

"Do you think that if you spend time in the society of persons with, let's put it no lower nor higher than this, certain inclinations and persuasions that that can cause an individual to change their values? Their perspectives, their innermost held views?"

"No, definitely not," said the vicar. I have my faith and that sustains me beyond temptations, however they may present themselves.

"What about you, Pettibum?"

Mr. Pettibone thought for a while and answered, "Vicar, that cocoa was first class; may I have another cup?"

"Certainly, Albert."

Coming back from the kitchen with the cup and saucer in hand, he said, "Here you are. Evensong will start soon, and I would really appreciate it if you would join the service. The parishioners would so much like to see you."

Reluctantly, Mr. Pettibone agreed to go. He was a confirmed atheist; his experiences had completely offset any need for superstition.

"Come along now, said the vicar, and Mr. Pettibone put his cup down and dutifully followed the vicar and the enthusiastic Mr. Palindrome.

'I wonder what's his game,' thought Mr. Pettibone as they processed into the pseudo-gothic structure of the church. Poorly lit, damp and cold, and with a sparse congregation, Mr. Pettibone took his seat in the place the vicar allocated, and was rather annoyed to find Palindrome sliding in next to him. Mr. Palindrome gave him a sideways leer, and then piously picked up the hymnal and joined with others as they sang the first hymn. His voice was surprisingly pleasant and he appeared to put real meaning into his singing. Mr. Pettibone considered but did not come to any different conclusion than his original.

Bored with what he considered meaningless mumbo jumbo, Mr. Pettibone fell into a sort of trance. He stood and sat as appropriate in a mechanical manner. At one point, his gaze fell on the altar piece; and then a second gaze. A third confirmed him in his suspicions. This could be and probably was a Geminiani Tryptich. It was not complete. There was one panel missing. That would be the one with the image of the Madonna. He knew where that panel was, although he had doubted its authenticity at the time. Perhaps he had made a mistake. A closer look at the triptych was necessary.

After the service, he asked the vicar whether he had any information about the altar piece. Nash replied that he did not have a clue. Palindrome was clearly interested but did not ask anything further.

"Did you know that could be a genuine Geminiani?" asked Mr. Pettibone.

"Valuable?" queried Palindrome.

"I'll say," replied Mr. Pettibone.

"It's all irrelevant to me," said the vicar. "Except that it's important as a focus for us to orientate our prayers and vows. Of course, I wouldn't know whether such a thing was otherwise of value, and its use to me is only as an object of adoration."

"Well, have you thought that if you were able to sell it, and if it were genuine, it might do a lot of good for the parish, not to say for the structure of the church. They always need something don't they, Vicar?"

Later that evening he had decided that further inspection was required. As an antiques' dealer, he found it useful to travel with a camera, to photograph items that might prove of interest. Consequently, he had brought his camera with him, a Leica with the ability to take detailed photographs under limited lighting. A thought also crossed his mind. If he were to be able to take a really good series of photographs, then he knew people, reliable and professional, who might make a very good copy. The vicar was clearly no judge of art, and it would be easy for him to return one day and make a substitution. Call it a nest egg for his old age.

The church was never locked, and so thinking, Mr. Pettibone carrying his camera jauntily made his way after he judged everyone to be in bed and snoring happily — including the dog and Mrs. Groynes, the housekeeper.

The first hurdle was that the church door was unexpectedly locked on this particular night. Somewhat perplexed, Mr. Pettibone stroked his chin and thought. Perhaps on learning that there might be a valuable item in the church, the vicar had prudently decided to secure the door. Undaunted, Mr. Pettibone took out a small leather pouch and from thence a few delicate instruments with which after a short while he was able to open the door. 'Amazing what one learns in prison,' he thought to himself, as he entered.

The church was completely dark and vacant but, despite this, welcoming. He tiptoed up to the altar aware that there was no human in the building. His keen senses told him that. Taking out a large flashlight from the leather bag that held his photographic equipment, he shone it at the altar.

With a start, he switched off the light and then sat down.
Switching on the light again, he careful inched it across the canvas, or where the canvas should have been. The Geminiani was not there. Someone had cut it from the frame.

'That bastard Palindrome' he thought. 'So that was what he was about.'

Gathering his things, he made his way back to the vicarage and to bed.

After a sleepless night, he came down to breakfast. The vicar looked up from his kedgeree.

"If you prefer bacon and eggs, please tell Mrs. Groynes in the kitchen. I am sure that she will be happy to fix you whatever you want."

"Palindrome not down yet?" asked Mr. Pettibone.

"Actually," said the vicar in between mouthfuls, "he left."

Mr. Pettibone said nothing and sat down at the table.

"What about breakfast?" asked the vicar.

"I'm not hungry," replied Mr. Pettibone. Shortly afterwards, he packed his things and was on his way back to London.

The following day, and with feelings that he could not adequately describe, Mr. Pettibone picked up the morning paper. On the second page there was an article that caught his attention:

Mystery of the missing vicar

The Vicar of Chelmsborough, a sleepy village in the west country appears to have gone missing. Without so much as a note to the Bishop and to the complete surprise of his housekeeper and the congregation, the Reverend Mr. Riordan Nash has disappeared off the face of the earth. Another mystery is the concomitant disappearance of the altar piece; the Bishop has suggested that although the two are clearly connected, he could not understand why anyone would want to take the lurid painting which was thought to be a late Victorian copy of a Geminiani artwork. And while foul play is not suspected, the police are anxious to interview two persons who were in the house with the vicar just before his disappearance.

"Well, I'll be damned!" exclaimed Mr. Pettibone, and let the paper fall to   the   floor.

Chapter 5: All Together Now

Mr. Pettibone was in an expansive mood. He had made a few excellent sales of furniture and paintings, some of the items genuine, others of more dubious authenticity. He felt flush and well-funded. As he walked across Holborn, he saw that the Empire was putting on a new review entitled, "All Together Now." This promised to be fun, and there would be all sorts of performers, including conjurors of various persuasions. He liked to watch them, as a prestidigitator (not a conjuror, you understand) of no mean prowess, it gave him great pleasure to unravel their tricks. He kept his findings to himself however, for as a considerate man, he did not want to spoil the fun for the audience.

"First class," he said to himself, "absolutely first class," and bought a ticket.

The house lights were up as he walked into the gilded auditorium that had seen so many famous music hall acts over the years. He had hazy memories of Harry Lauder, Marie Lloyd, and Dan Leno. He liked to imagine that his Mum had taken him to see them. Highly unlikely, he reflected; they wouldn't have had enough money for such frivolities. But he did now, and beaming his beneficent smile, he gazed out over the audience to see if there was anyone whom he recognized. Not a sausage, and he squeezed his sausage-like body into the faded red plush chair and admired the Edwardian glory of this amazing house. A blousy lady sat next to him, and repeatedly enveloped him with her feather boa, as she tried to adjust it over her copious bosom.

"Oh, do excuse me," she said looking him directly in the eye.

Was she propositioning him, he wondered, but when a man, obviously her husband, pranced up and sat down right next to her he thought, 'No such luck!' But even this was not a disappointment to a man who had experienced such a profitable day. And the money he made was burning a hole in his breast pocket. In truth, although Mr. Pettibone liked to think of himself as frugal, in actuality he had reached a point in his life when he could deny himself nothing.

"Nothing but the best; that's what you deserve, my boy." His father's words reverberated in his head as the orchestra struck up the overture to the show. During a particularly moving part of the music, Mr. Pettibone recollected that the advice was as hollow as his father's savings.

The lights dimmed and the first act started. Mr. Pettibone promptly fell asleep. He had dined rather well at a chop house and also accompanied the meal with copious amounts of stout, of which he was abundantly fond. He had often thought dismally how appropriate the nomenclature of such beer was: not only was it stout in itself but it ensured that worthy quality in those who drank it. He woke up a short while later, as the blousy woman next to him dug him sharply in the ribs.

"Shush, and stop snoring," she said and fixed him with a malevolent expression.

"Sorry," said a contrite Mr. Pettibone. He had missed the first act altogether, but was now fully awake for the second. It promised to be absolutely first-class, since it was listed in the program, which he clutched in his pudgy fist, as:

Dr. 'Stinker' Malvern MA (Oxon) the Academic Prestidigitator.

"Well, streuth," he said, and a soft whistle escaped from his lips. The lady next to him, again dug him sharply in the ribs. He turned to her and softly whispered in her ear, "Madame, if you do that again, you won't be needing a dentist anymore."

The curtain went up, and so did Mr. Pettibone, or at least he half rose in his chair in surprise. In front of him, in threadbare full evening dress, and MA gown of equal antiquity, was the unmistakable personage of the Reverend Riordan Nash.

Mr. Pettibone was too amazed to pay attention to what his reverence was doing on stage, but kept on muttering, "Well, I never. Blimey."

The stout lady disdained to look at him, and wisely refrained from digging Mr. Pettibone in the ribs. Clearly, she wanted to retain her dentition.

"So that's how the bugger ended up." It was nearly three years since their last encounter. The Rev. Mr. Nash had made off with the Geminiani triptych — or at least the two parts of it — and apparently disappeared off the face of the earth. And now here he was in all his glory — Dr. 'Stinker' Malvern MA(Oxon) — for all to see. However, the audience did not think him divine, greeting the end of his performance with muted applause mingled with the appreciative raspberry. Dr. 'Stinker' bowed to the audience, and barely stifled a belch as he departed the stage. There was no curtain call.

In the interval, Mr. Pettibone got up and after conscientiously treading on the stout lady's feet found himself in the aisle. He asked an usher for directions to the performers' dressing rooms, and after a small amount of cash changed hands, the usher provided the appropriate answer.

Making his way down a series of narrow, dirty cream-coloured corridors at the back of the theatre dimly lit with naked light bulbs, he eventually came to a room with a sign indicating that its current occupant was likely to be 'Stinker' Malvern. He politely knocked on the door, and was greeted with a booming, and none too sober sounding, "Piss off. I'm busy."

The accent, however, was unmistakably refined. Obviously, the seminary had taught Mr. Nash a thing or two. Or was it Oxford? Mr. Pettibone was too flabbergasted to think that one through. Despite the intensity of the welcome, Mr. Pettibone boldly opened the door and found a dejected-looking Nash sitting in front of his make-up mirror, glass in hand.

"Do I know you?" he asked. And putting the glass of brandy down stared and then exclaimed:

"Upon my soul, it's Pettibone! I am pleased to see you. Did you see my act?"

"Oh, yes," said Mr. Pettibone.

"Well, what did you think?"

"First class, absolutely first class," Mr. Pettibone lied.

"Did you recognize the tricks? They were mostly ones you taught me in the Scrubs."

Mr. Pettibone did not reply, and looking down at the floor he mumbled, "I am so sorry to see you like this, Mr. Nash."

"Oh, don't be. I was tempted, and I yielded. The Bishop was very kind, especially as I confessed and volunteered to make reparations. But he made it clear he felt my association with convicts for so many of my early clerical years had turned my head. I was not a good candidate for the cloth; so I was unfrocked. And then unemployed; and then unemployable. No police record, fortunately, but no references either. Do you think that I just have an evil streak, or am I too easily influenced by others, Mr. Pettibone?"

"Couldn't say, Vicar. Couldn't say."

"You can't call me that. My new vocation is sleight of hand; and I don't mind in the slightest. It is a relief in some ways. I don't have to carry the burden of others' sins. Only my own. Only my own," he repeated sadly and took another sip of brandy.

"Is there anything I can do?" asked Pettibone.

"Not at all. You have given me a great gift already. Your education has proven far more useful than the one that I got at Oxford." And he laughed a mirthless laugh.

Mr. Pettibone could not ascertain whether Nash was feeling sorry for himself or had genuinely decided to try fresh fields and pastures new.

Reaching inside his pocket, Mr. Pettibone retrieved a somewhat dog-eared visiting card.

"You may have lost my address and phone number, but here it is again. If you need anything, let me know."

"Thank you," said Nash, "but it's time for me to stand on my own two feet. Although I have sinned, I haven't fallen. Not completely. I still believe in God."

"I don't," said Mr. Pettibone. "I think that being a prestidigitator is no more than a continuation of your old job. All that transubstantiation stuff. Nothing more than psychological trickery."

"That is the saddest thing I have heard for a long time," said Mr. Nash. "I really don't know what I would do without my faith. Besides, I think that you have the wrong denomination there."

"But don't you think God should have stopped you from doing all of this?"

"I still pray, Mr. Pettibone."

"But is there anyone listening, Mr. Nash?" Mr. Pettibone replied and then realized that perhaps he had been unnecessarily cruel.

"There is always someone listening. And if you are patient, answering. You see, I believe that we are constantly given moral choices by God each day and that we have the free will to choose. What we do is up to us. But we have to accept the consequences of our bad choices, if we make them. I think that is the essence of being human."

"And can you redeem yourself, Vicar?"

"I hope so. Oh, God, I really hope so."

"Well goodbye, Vicar," said Mr. Pettibone, "and don't lose the card."

"God be with you," said Mr. Nash, and took another sip of brandy as Mr. Pettibone softly closed the door.

A few days later Mr. Pettibone found himself outside Christianson, the famous London auction house. He knew that there was a sale on today but had somehow lost interest for the moment. The interview with Mr. Nash, or 'Stinker' Malvern as he had come to be called, had demoralized him. His good mood at the start of that evening had evaporated as substantially as it had come, and not yet returned. Still, he entered the august building and purchased the listing, hoping eventually to be distracted for a few hours. The auction had started, and Mr. Pettibone slowly became captivated by the atmosphere. The thrill of the chase, he thought. High up on a side wall, and somewhat in the shadows, he saw with a start three familiar paintings. Two of them were clearly from the church at Chelmsborough, and the third was obviously the property of Mr. Stokes. Looking around, he saw the slight figure of Timothy Stokes at the back of the room, and he nodded, but did not think that Timothy had seen him. The paintings were listed as:

School of Federico D'Este Geminiani 'The Master of Padua.' Three paintings to be sold variously in consecutive lots.

One was stated as "the property of a gentleman;" the other two were not attributed to any individual person, but the provenance was written up as:

Derequisitioned by the Church of England. Surplus to requirement.

Mr. Pettibone thought that was rather a comment on himself and laughed a little. And what indeed if they turned out to be genuine? At the time, Mr. Pettibone was somewhat sure of the lack of authenticity of the first, and the Bishop had been advised that the remainder of the triptych was also dubious. Mr. Pettibone had not had the inclination to do the research that was necessary to establish authenticity and had devoted his time to other matters. But whatever the issue, would it not be a good idea to look at all three together. Reunited. Whether real or false, fact or fiction. And did it matter? Looking up again at the three pieces, he knew that they were beautiful, who ever had made them. A warm feeling crept into his heart, and he felt a slight shudder of grief. Suffering, that was what it was all about.

The numeration showed that they were likely to come up for sale in the late afternoon. Mr. Pettibone had not intended to stay, but felt a compulsion to see what interest there actually might be in the Geminiani triptych. Would anyone recognize that they belonged together? The auction house had separated the panels and hung them poorly in the shadows and out of sequence. He stayed and waited. In the late afternoon, the items were displayed and the auctioneer started the bidding. To Mr. Pettibone's dismay there was considerable interest and the bidding soon reached proportions that he thought unjustified even if the paintings were genuine. He continued to bid, and with his heart racing, bid further. Up and up went the bids until eventually, and with a face covered in perspiration, Mr. Pettibone could sit back in his chair, victorious. It would take all the money he had made the other day from his own sales of items genuine and those perhaps of dubious authenticity. Just like the Geminiani, he thought. He would also have to dig hard into his savings to cover the remainder. But it was worth it. Just to see the three panels together. And in his mind's eye, he saw the complete work, and he wept. Not with triumph but with a new feeling that he could not completely understand.

After the sale, he went to the back office and some time later was met by a dutiful attendant. Mr. Pettibone shakily took out his cheque book and inked in the details, and lastly the large sum he was paying.

"And what, Sir, might be the delivery address? And the name of the recipient? Shall it be yourself, Sir?"

Mr. Pettibone thought for a while and wrote:

> To: The Priest in Charge
> Chelmsborough Church
> Chelmsborough, Stanx

And on a card, he wrote:

> With the Compliments of Mr. Riordan Nash, Sometime Vicar of this Parish.

And on a separate card with only the rubric:

> Pettibone, Sons and Langford, Dealers and Valuers of Fine Antiques

he wrote: Without any question, this is a genuine Geminiani Triptych.

He put his pen away vowing to justify these words with thorough research and to provide the Bishop with the details.

Looking at the cheque, the young attendant turned to Mr. Pettibone.

"That is a staggering amount for a Geminiani, Sir. I hope you think it worth it."

"Yes," said Mr. Pettibone. "Yes, I rather think it is."

Part III: I'll Be Seeing You

Chapter 1: Number 12

Mr. Edwards was a 'family man', or at least he would have been if he had one. But to his despair, he never really found the opportunity. Life had got in the way; well, a sort of life, and actually one in which he had even been quite successful. Coming from a middle-class family in the midlands, he found himself at an early age in charge of the family paint manufacturing business. With acumen, foresight, and some degree of courage, he had maneuvered it into a national concern of some merit and substance. He was now on his way to London to finalize the deal.

To tell the truth, he was in two minds about it. An Italian conglomerate made a substantial offer, and he had accepted. It would make him even more rich. As he sat in the back of his car and Gregory his driver was entering the outskirts of London via the North Circular Road, he pondered why he was selling. Well, he thought, times were changing, and he found that at his age, 67, he could no longer change with them.

On the other hand, what would he do with all the money? He had no children and no close relatives. He settled back in the cushions of his car and thought.

Entering the last part of the journey to the hotel, Gregory asked Mr. Edwards whether he would need the car during his stay in London. Given the reliable, albeit uncomfortable public transport system, he gave him the week off. Mr. Edwards was not a fan of London. In fact, he tried to avoid the city as much as possible; but now as he was here, perhaps he could use the time to go to the opera, put in a concert and definitely see a play or two. And even a game of football. He picked up

The Times and turned to the entertainment section; one or two things did catch his eye, and he made a note to ask the concierge at the Dorset to book seats for the following Monday and Tuesday.

The doorman greeted Mr. Edwards with an ingratiating smile as he stepped out of his car.

"Welcome to the Dorset, Sir," he said as he held the door. A blast of hot air greeted Mr. Edwards, and he flexed his shoulders involuntarily. This was a standard London February day, cold and damp, and the sudden blast came as a shock.

"Welcome, Mr. Edwards. So nice to see you again," said the concierge. Mr. Edwards was surprised. When in London, he always stayed at the Dorset, although the last time was about five years ago. He squinted hard, being somewhat short of sight and too vain to wear glasses, he could not recognize the smiling face in front of him. "Here is your key. Room 12 as usual."

Going to the lift with the porter who piled his luggage on some sort of contraption adapted for the purpose — for Mr. Edwards did not travel light — he recognized the familiar smells and decorations. The quietness, sound deadened by the thick, plush carpets. The tasteful and subtle, but very costly brocades and wood. And above all, the vases filled with flowers. On his way to the lift, Mr. Edwards could not resist the urge to touch the leaves to see if they were genuine. They were.

"Here we are, Sir," and Mr. Edwards smiled at the "we." He delighted in the cozy comfort exuded by the furnishings. Everything was as he remembered it. And if he had to come to the 'Great Wen', he wanted to be cozy, and he made sure that nothing could spoil it. From the street, there was little to be heard. The windows closed with a perfect fit, unusual in this post-war period, and there was mainly foot traffic he noted as he stepped to the window and looked out over the gloomy Mayfair Street. It was beginning to spit.

A good dinner at the hotel restaurant comprising a mock turtle soup (with sherry), followed by lemon (not Dover) sole, and beef Wellington with a bavarois to follow, and then a good cognac. He sat in the smoking room, enjoying his cigar and coffee, and trying to finish the evening paper. It was Friday, business on Monday, and in the intervening weekend, what was he to do? There was nothing on in town that took his fancy. And then his gaze stopped at a small advertisement:

"Bored? Why not come down to Portobello Road? We have hundreds of stalls. You might find that very thing you have been looking for all your life (and we don't mean a wife!)."

He remembered being taken there as a child, a small boy of 7, bored (indeed) while his parents, avid collectors of this and that, bought a large collection of early nineteenth-century aquatints of London. They hung in the first-floor landing stairwell of his house, and he hated them. Perhaps that's when his antipathy to London started, cemented by his parents sending him to school there. A most disagreeable experience.

He woke on Saturday, and, drawing the curtains back to reveal a drizzly morning, he thought he would go to the Portobello market. The concierge was not particularly impressed when he asked for directions and suggested instead a visit to a porcelain exhibition at the V&A. But for some reason, Mr. Edwards was not inclined, and within a few hours there he was standing in the rain, at the top of Portobello Road surveying the scene below.

Full of ambling prospects, the people shoved each other this way and that to get a closer look at the items on display. Given the rain, some of the stalls, although covered, had further drawn sheets of polythene over their merchandise. He expected to see the usual rubbish: 'What passes as antique these days,' he thought, 'would have been classified as junk in my day, and we would have had to pay the dustmen to cart the stuff away.'

To his amazement, although there were items of lesser interest, there were scattered among them some genuinely fascinating objects. After walking down half one side of the street, and venturing into the adjacent houses that had been turned into shops, his stomach told him it was time for lunch. And so he sauntered into a pub, called the "In a Glass Darkly" and ordered a ploughman's lunch and a pint of stout.

An hour later, feeling that all was well with the world, he sauntered out of the pub. It had stopped raining. His shortsightedness was a problem; perhaps it was the stout allowing him to overcome his vanity for he now wondered whether he could find some frames here. Good gold (solid, not plated). Ones that he could have filled with his prescription. He walked down the rest of that side of the road and then crossed to go up towards the tube station at the top. At the second stall, displayed for his viewing pleasure, was a selection of antique spectacle frames. There must have been at least a hundred. All shapes and sizes: square, round, hexagonal, half-moon; in steel, silver and gold plate, and then in a locked box, solid gold and silver. All periods were represented, with the earliest ones being small and round. He wondered how they ever stayed on anyone's face. He asked the stall owner.

"Had an elastic fastener in the back, Gov. That's why there are these holes." The man took up a pair and showed Mr. Edwards who looked at him appraisingly. The stall holder was probably in his late fifties, with very long, dirty, grey hair that hung in curled-up ringlets around his neck and over his forehead. He was fat, with pudgy fingers that however moved with surgical precision and great grace as they handed frames sequentially over to Mr. Edwards for his inspection.

He was dressed in a short raincoat open at the front, under which was a grey pullover decorated with moth holes of alarmingly large dimensions. Beneath were several other layers. Mr. Edwards wondered looking at him whether instead of washing each morning, he just put on an extra set of clothing, until at the end of the week he peeled off the whole lot and washed them.

He looked at the case and suddenly saw exactly what he wanted. "I want to see those, please." His eyes had landed on a beautiful pair of engraved gold glasses, mid-nineteenth century. He tried them on, and not only did they fit, but as he looked through the lenses he was surprised at the clarity of what he could see. The sun had come out and the people had vanished. Odd, he thought, as he took the glasses off and handed them back to the dealer. As he did so, he noted that it had started to rain again and the street was packed. Odd, he thought again.

"They suit you," said the stall keeper.

"I'll take them," said Mr. Edwards. When told the substantial figure, he nodded, pulled his wallet out of his breast pocket, and paid without demur. The dealer looked at him with astonishment; normally, there would be some haggling over price, a little dance that he relished. In the end, after significant hand waving and expressions of how each was fleecing the other, both parties would settle and be happy. But not this time. Ruefully the dealer put the glasses into a gold spectacle case that came with them and handed them to Mr. Edwards. His day was ruined, and after Mr. Edwards left, he closed the stall and headed to the pub to console himself over a pint or five.

On the way back to his hotel, Mr. Edwards stopped off at an old-fashioned chop house and ordered his dinner. A bottle of claret helped him digest the lamb chops, which followed the brown Windsor soup and was completed with a plum pudding and port and three cups of a dark sticky fluid supposed to be coffee.

On the way out of the restaurant, he fumbled in his pocket and retrieved the gold glasses, maneuvering them on to his nose. In front of him now, was an organ grinder and a monkey on a chain, although they were rather indistinct in the gaslight. But, thought Mr. Edwards, I was under the impression that there was a law against all of this. And what also troubled him was that although the organ grinder was grinding away at a furious pace, no sound reached his ears. It was deathly silent. The monkey was jumping up and down and had leapt towards him, holding a greasy cap in its outstretched hand. Mr. Edwards took a step back, regained his balance and took the glasses off. The organ grinder and his monkey had vanished, and the gaslight replaced by the yellow of the sodium lamps gave the empty road a bilious appearance.

"Indigestion," said Mr. Edwards, "clearly I have eaten too much," and his stomach rumbled loudly in agreement.

Returning to his hotel somewhat later than he had expected, he walked down the silent, dim corridor to his room. He could not make out the room numbers clearly and put on the glasses again. At the door of Number 12, he paused. A sense of ill ease had swept over him. Unusual, as Mr. Edwards was not a man of fancies, rather a hard-headed businessman. This time though, he thought he could hear muffled voices. "Must be from next door," he said to himself as he opened the door to the room. Inside, directly in front of him and completely ignoring his entrance, stood a man and a woman arguing.

Mr. Edwards was mesmerized. They were in their twenties, an attractive couple, dressed in contemporary clothes. The woman was in red, and the man had a scar on the left side of his face. The man suddenly raised his arm and Mr. Edwards saw what looked like a knife in his hand. The woman sank to the ground and seemed to be imploring him not to kill her. And then suddenly she rose and confronted the man. A vase behind her crashed to the ground as she did so, and the flowers and water spilled onto the patterned carpet. The man stopped in his tracks.

Mr. Edwards thought he had clearly entered the wrong room. He did not want to be involved in a scene, especially a violent one like this, although he was a courageous soul. He just had a horror of emotional scenes. So his immediate reaction was to step back and close the door softly. In doing so, he took off the gold glasses, took in a breath and chose to overcome his reluctance to put a stop to this deplorable event. Without much resistance, the door flew open at his overwrought pressure; the room was completely empty. In the near distance, he could see that the bed had been turned down and the decanter of whiskey that the management placed for his convenience had been filled. The flowers he had just seen strewn all over the floor were back in the vase, and the vase was back on the table.

"Streuth," said Mr. Edwards, completely at a loss. "Something wrong with my eyesight, definitely," and he tossed the gold spectacles now back in their case onto an armoire. They hit the edge and slipped down onto the floor where they stayed hidden by a chair. "Something odd here," he said to himself as he undressed. He had suffered a shock and was completely at a loss to explain it.

"There's something about this room. And not my indigestion," he said, and his rumbling stomach tried to tell him otherwise. He got up and poured himself a helpful tumbler of whiskey and thought through things.

"You know, old boy, I think that you are slowly going batty. Too much time on your hands. What are you going to do when you have sold the firm? Go on a world cruise? Yuck!"

Mr. Edwards was not a fanciful man, and he lacked any trace of imagination. "Yes, I'm slowly going crazy," and he shook his head sadly. "What you need is aim and purpose. Aim and purpose, my boy," he repeated. And hadn't his father said the same thing to him all those years ago, when suggesting that he join the family firm? He fell asleep at last.

On waking the next morning, everything was clear and he had made up his mind. He called his driver on the telephone and told him to be at the main entrance of the hotel at 10:30 sharp. After breakfast, he settled his bill and handed in the room key.

"I'm sorry you are leaving us early," said the concierge. "I hope that your stay was satisfactory?"

"Yes, yes indeed," he replied. He decided that in no circumstances was he going to sell the firm and sent several telegrams to that effect. Everything would remain the same, just as it should be.

After leaving the dining room and collecting a *Financial Times* (weekend edition) on the way out, he saw Gregory in the distance and waved to him. Mr. Edwards initially paid little attention to the young couple who entered, but then stopped to take a closer look because there was something familiar about them. He reached in his pocket for the gold glasses, but could not find them. He shrugged his shoulders. "Lost them, I shouldn't wonder," he said to himself, "and good riddance is what I say."

He entered the car, just as the man with the scar on the left side of his face and his pretty wife in the red dress were standing at the counter.

"Number 12," said the concierge, and handed them the key.

Chapter 2: 'Til Death Do Us Part

Mrs. Samuels was a rather blousy woman and one with the characteristic great heart of her type. She was addicted to mascara and also hair spray, but generally looked as immaculate as she possibly could as long as her bra straps didn't show. On occasions she was aware that people found her amusing, not her jokes but just she herself. Was it what she said? She knew that sometimes she might not come out with the best response to something emotional or deeply felt, but she did feel deeply. For herself and for others. And she was generous to a fault.

Gentlemen at the local pub often bought her drinks, even more so in the past two years since Tom passed. Her darling husband. They had been married for nearly fifty years, when he needs must have a heart attack and dropped dead right in front of her. Right in the middle of the best room, the parlor at the front of the house. Thank heavens they weren't expecting company, she thought as she viewed his stiffening corpse. Funny what comes into your mind when confronted with the unimaginable. And then she dissolved into hysterics, which lasted nearly two years.

She found the attentions of Fred, the next-door neighbour, pleasant, but truth to tell, he was married and she was not inclined. Not only not inclined, but incapable. Her love for Tom grew instead of diminished, and the aching sense of loss could not be assuaged. She glanced at herself in the makeup mirror as she carefully applied bright red lipstick. Nice of her daughter to invite her for dinner. Sarah was as much upset by her father's death as Mrs. Samuels, but as time passed, she seemed to adjust and she certainly was able to get on with her life.

Well, she had a job, didn't she, and a lazy husband and two small boys. They took up all her time, while Mrs. Samuels had a cat, and Kitty was now curled lovingly in her well upholstered lap during the ongoing process of titivation.

It was her birthday, and Sarah had at last invited her for dinner. The first time in nearly eight months. Should she say something? But Mrs. Samuels was afraid that in her unintentionally blunt way, something would be said that she would regret, and that would be that. She looked at the wilting flowers on her dressing table that she bought to take to her daughter's that night. 'It will do,' she thought, although the colors were rapidly fading. "Rather like me," she mused dismally as she applied another coating of blush with the thick camel-hair brush.

She rang the doorbell of the semi-detached house, or villa as the Victorians had originally called such modest accommodation, when not attached to 200 others on a terrace. Trevor, her 12-year-old grandson, opened the door. She peered into the pimpled face and tried to see whether there was any resemblance to Tom.

Undecided on this issue, she stepped inside just in time to hear Oliver, her son-in-law, ask her daughter, "When is your mother coming? She should be here by now and I promised I'd be at the pub at 9. The lads have set up a game of darts."

"Olly, you know she misses Dad."

"Gran's here!" shouted Trev excitedly. "Did you bring me a present, Gran?" he asked eagerly.

"Not this time, dear. But if you're a good boy this evening, you never know, I might have to give you a reward. Where's Robert?" She never used Rob, but always Robert for the younger son. Abbreviated names were common, she thought. Vulgar.

"Oh, Rob's in bed. It's past his bedtime," said her daughter coming out of the kitchen and rubbing her hands on a tea towel as she bent forward to kiss her mother. "But go upstairs and say goodnight. I know he'll want to see you." She went and he did.

Coming downstairs, avoiding the toys strewn on the steps and thinking, "don't want to fall at my age. Might break a hip. And then where would I be? Probably with Tom," she thought, and sadly kicked a bright yellow, plastic truck down the stairs.

"Cheer up, Mum," said Sarah, "it is your birthday. And we have a few surprises for you."

"Yes," said Oliver, and obviously proud of himself he continued, "I've got a job."

"About high time," said Mrs. Samuels, and regretted the words as soon as they were out. Oliver looked down, and forcing a smile said to himself, "silly old cow!"

Trying to make up for her indiscretion, upon being told that he was going to work in the electric shop down the road and was learning to repair toasters, Mrs. Samuels told them how delighted she was for them. And in her general way overdid the praise, as she had overdone the make-up that evening.

"And of course, Mum, we have a present for you, don't we Olly?" Mrs. Samuels winced at the epithet. "Give it to her, Olly," and Oliver wasn't sure exactly what he should give her, a piece of his mind for turning his wife into a snob, or a knuckle sandwich? "Oh, righty," he said, and got up and retrieved the parcel.

"Trev wrapped it himself," he said, and thrust the parcel out as if it were a bomb about to explode.

"I did," said Trevor proudly.

"From us all," said Sarah. The parcel hardly needed to be unwrapped. Whatever was in it was barely hidden by the wrapping paper that proclaimed: "Merry Christmas." Seeing Mrs. Samuels' expression, Sarah said, "I know, Mum, but we're going through a difficult patch."

"Oh, it doesn't matter, reeelly it doesn't," said Mrs. Samuels. And they couldn't even go to the bother of buying one measly sheet of birthday paper. Now if Tom were alive ... she thought. And indeed, if Tom were alive things would have been different. He wouldn't have tolerated anything that even suggested an insult to his wife. And he would have let anyone know. Perhaps that's where she learned to be a little more forthright in her replies than was good for her, she wondered.

"Anyway," she said as the wrapping paper fell away at her touch, "it's the thought that counts." As she took out the cardboard box, she wondered whether there really was any thought behind the gift. I might as well be kind, she said to herself and opened the box. Perplexed, she took out a pair of gold eyeglasses.

"Real gold they are, Mum," said her daughter. "Try them on."

"Bought them at the pub, I did. Cost me a fair bit I can tell you. Nothing too good for you, Mum," Oliver said, with just a hint of sarcasm. "Gladys works at that posh hotel in London. The Dorset. She found them under a cupboard. No-one asked for them, so she thought …"

"I know what she thought," said Mrs. Samuels, her tongue getting the better of her.

"Well, if you don't want them …" said Sarah sharply.

But Mrs. Samuels was now admiring herself in the mirror.

"They look really good on me, don't they? "And you know, they're a perfect prescription. Don't think I need to go to the opticians to get them adjusted. Thank you, pet," she said to Sarah, "and you, Oliver … Olly," she forced herself to add.

And despite the initial awkwardness, the rest of the evening went well. Oliver and Trevor behaved themselves. Sarah said, as she saw her mother into the minicab, "I know I should invite you over more often. But with the kids, the job, and Olly …"

"I know," said Mrs. Samuels, and settled her capacious buttocks onto the capacious seating at the back of the car. "Don't worry. And I've got these new specs," she said waving the gold case in the air.

"See you through the week, they will," and they both laughed.

Mr. Siddiqui, the driver, asked for the address and off they went. On reaching home, Mrs. Samuels was met by an angry, black cat. She had forgotten to feed Kitty. She opened the cupboard where she kept all her cleaning stuff and the cat's food, but the light didn't come on when she turned the switch.

"Bother," said Mrs. Samuels. She never swore. "Perhaps these will help," and she put on the gold spectacles. They didn't quite fit, and slid down her nose a little. In the time that she saw over the lenses she was able to discern the tins of cat food and picked one up to give to Kitty. As she turned 'round, she pushed the glasses up onto the bridge of her nose.

"Hello, Sheila," said Tom. "I've missed you."

Mrs. Samuels dropped the cat food and Kitty ran off at the shock of the sound of tin on wood.

"TOM!"

"Yes. It's me. Don't look so shocked. I've been here all the time, only you couldn't see me. I've tried so hard to get your attention, but you didn't hear or see."

"But was it you and the running toilet?"

"No. Of course not, you silly thing. But the broken cat vase. That was me. I so wanted to talk to you. I could see that you were upset after the funeral and all. I wanted to let you know that everything was okay."

"Except that it wasn't, Tom. I will never get over it."

"But you must. It isn't healthy."

"I love you so much," she said.

"Love or loved?"

"Love, always will."

"I love you, too," said Tom. "And that's why I'm still here. Just to see you even if you don't see me. But I'm sorry that you've had such a bad time. You need to get on with your life."

"I can't. I won't. And you can't either. That's why you're still here, isn't it?" she said.

"Well, yes. I want to protect you, save you."

"Save me! From what?"

"From yourself. Being so cooped up, and also hasn't your tongue got a little sharper? I think that it's time you found a new husband."

"Don't be daft," said Mrs. Samuels.

"Go on, girl. It'll do you good. And you're still not bad-looking. Put on a few pounds perhaps, but there's many would like a little something to keep them warm these winter months."

"Don't be crude, Tom."

Tom closed his eyes, and then said, "There's something I want to find out."

"Yes?"

"Did you ever know?"

Mrs. Samuels looked away and then down at her feet.

"You know it didn't mean anything."

"Is that what you're here to say, Tom?"

"Yes. It's been on my mind. Did you know?"

"Of course I did. A wife, and with our love, of course I knew. Anyone would."

"I'm so sorry," Tom said, with real pain in his voice.

"Oh, don't be. Was it only one?" She asked, but she thought she knew the answer. He did not reply.

"Well, it's all water under the bridge now." She picked at the front of her blouse and her agitation grew. She was a mixture of emotions.

"Tom, will you stay?"

"I don't know. It depends. If you forgive me …"

"There's nothing to forgive."

"It's been on my mind for all these years. Since the first time."

"I know. You men. After a while, things get a little stale and you look for something else."

"I tell you there's only been you. All I could think of was you. And our girl Sarah … The others, they meant nothing," Tom said.

"They…?" she asked, but of course she had been clear about these little diversions. After the first one, which occurred within the second year of their marriage, she knew he needed these dalliances. Wasn't that what the Victorians called an affair? He needed them, and she needed him. She could forgive him anything, and she had. She never let on that she knew. And because of that it had still been a wonderful marriage. And together they had a daughter. But did he have other children? With so many dalliances over the years, it was inevitable, wasn't it? She started to shake. That would make a difference, definitely, she thought. She wondered why she had never thought of finding out before.

"Tom, is Sarah your only child?"
A pause. "No," he said.

"How many?"

"Three … well five, counting the twins."

"Did you keep up with them?"

"No. Well, not really, not often, only occasionally like. Of course, Eileen wanted …"

"Eileen. That slag," shouted Mrs. Samuels.

"She wasn't that bad. And I gave her some cash and that was alright. Around then she married Ernie and told him it was his."

"He believed her?"

"He half believed her, but he loved the child. And why make matters worse?"

"Why, indeed?" mused Mrs. Samuels.

And now that he was here, not physically but in spirit, she was beginning to see. And strangely enough, to feel the emotions she had repressed for so long. She wiped the tears from behind the glasses.

"The other women?"

"Beryl ..."

"Not that one, Tom, surely not? Don't you have any taste, any pride?"

"We'd had a little tiff, you and me, and I was feeling cross. Beryl, she's very accommodating ..."

"I'll say!

"And soon after, Beryl had the twins. Nice lads, really good boys. I'm proud of them."

"And what about Sarah?"

"I'm proud of her too. But ..."

"But you always wanted a boy. Someone to talk to when he grew up."

"Yes, I suppose so," Tom said wistfully.

"You know, Tom, I really loved you."

"And I love you."

"I *loved* you," she repeated, emphasizing the past tense, "and I think I always will be fond of you, now. But being that you're not here ..."

"But I am, darling. I'm here, and I'll always be here," Tom said.

"Those twins. Who looked after them? Beryl could hardly have been a good mother."

"She gave them to her sister to look after. They couldn't have kids. A nice home, and they grew up to think that her sister and husband were their real parents. I would go over from time to time."

"Oh, I suppose, good old Uncle Tom."

"But you said you knew."

"I knew there was more than one woman. I didn't know about the kids!"

"And that makes a difference?"

"That makes a difference."

"But why?"

"I don't know, but it does."

"You said you forgave me."

"I know I did."

"Do you?"

She did not reply.

"Do you?" The repetition was almost a plea.

She still did not reply, unsure as to how to answer. Tears were starting to flow again, and she took off the glasses to wipe her eyes. When she looked ahead again, Tom had vanished. She put them on again, and he was standing in front of her with a look of such contrition. She almost …

She took the glasses off and he had gone again.

"Til death do us part," she said, and threw the glasses into a box marked, "Oxfam."

Chapter 3: Forty Years On.

It'll be okay, I promise you," said his wife.

He wasn't so sure. He never liked going back. He knew there were many who did. But why bring back old memories; of course, if they were good ones, that might be different. But were his? He thought he knew.

The small inn in the village had been there since time immemorial, and as there was nowhere else to stay in the neighborhood, all of the boys' parents had at one time or another passed through its Tudor doors. And then up its creaking steps to a drafty, sparse bedroom. With chamber pot. For this, and for the resident ghost, the patrons were asked to shell out a larger amount of money than the accommodation was worth. But it was worth it, as it was so close to the school.

The parents were generally proud that their offspring studied at such a well-regarded establishment, and well-regarded it was since its foundation in the thirteenth century. Or was it the fourteenth or perhaps the fifteenth? Well, he didn't remember and frankly didn't care. He had hated most of his time there. Dorchester School had been a real pain. Actually, the boys never called it by that name; it was always "Duster," a corruption from the local dialect.

Like many such boarding establishments, it sat sequestered away from significant human habitation, much like a leper colony.

"Julian," she said, "I am so looking forward to meeting your friends."

Julia was his third wife. They had been married a few years, a few happy years, and it was she who insisted on his coming to this event. He knew that most wives worth their salt were intrigued by their husbands' past lives, all the better to understand and be a part of them. Admirable, he thought, but he had no such interest. Julia was a world in herself, and he took her as she was, and to hell with any past. If there was any. And rather like his attitude to the history of that august establishment where he had been invited back on the fortieth anniversary of setting foot there, he could not have cared less. However, he was a caring person at heart. And he cared very much for his wife. That was why, against his better judgment, they were here.

Julia and Julian, he thought. That will cause some interesting comments and he wondered whether there might be a suitable Latin epigram that he could use. His query was unanswered.

He recalled the last time he went to one of these events, Founders' Days they were called, and the annual tribute to Henry II, or was it VI, who had conjured the dreadful idea of instituting this school — for the poor, would you believe? — to safeguard his soul in the hereafter. It had been a disaster. His old headmaster had buttonholed him for half an hour, regaling him with tales from the sickbed. The heart attack had been bad but he had survived to tell the tale (and go on to torment another generation of innocents parenthetically thought Julian). "Oh, what he had been through," the headmaster sighed, but it had given him a new respect for the medical profession. Julian James yawned, discretely. "Yes, Sir," he said. Then further tales of an operation exhaustingly followed.

"I thought you would be interested, James, with you being a medical man and such," the headmaster said. 'No,' Julian thought, 'I could not be less interested in the state of your guts. In fact, I hate them as much now as I did then. Well, what could you expect from a mathematician? A classicist would have at least had class.'

"Julian, hurry up or we'll be late. And put on those glasses; they make you look so distinguished," Julia said.

Which they did. Julia had bought them in an Oxfam shop as they had intrigued her. She thought that they might be real gold, and when she had cleaned and polished them, they turned out to be just that.

"And all for five pounds," she had said proudly; and if there was anything that Julia was proud of it was a bargain.

"These beastly drafts," he complained. "They haven't changed. Nothing has, more's the pity!" He remembered his first day. His prep school had not been boarding; he had been a little too weak for that, bad chest and other ailments, but as he had recovered, his parents decided to send him away to the same school they had sent his elder brother. That brother had regaled him at night with tales of the most horrific about what they did to new boys, and Julian had recoiled in horror.

"I'm not going. No!" He shrieked when kitted out in his uniform, made for him at Rowe's on Bond Street. He had stood in the hall, alone and waiting for the driver to take him to the station. His nurse, who was still with the family (actually more or less one of the family) had told him to think himself lucky. Hadn't so many famous men come from that school? And the fees?

"No, Nanny Pat. It's awful. I don't want to go. I don't want to leave you."

"Master Julian, it's about time that you grew up. You can't always be tied to my coattails or those of your mother for that matter."

And where were his parents? In Switzerland with their friends on a skiing holiday. And they had left him here when he was to go to that hell, without even being there to say goodbye to him. His father, a somewhat remote, genial, but superficial man had patted him on the back, given him a fiver and told him not to hesitate to ask for more if he needed it.

"When I was at Duster, all you needed to make yourself popular was cash, and a hamper, and we will send that to you from Fortnums every month, won't we dear?" he asked his wife.

"I suppose so," said Lady Julia, after whom he had been named in a fit of uncharacteristic emotion.

And off he had gone, most reluctantly, in the front seat of the car, sandwiched between the driver and Nanny Pat so that he had no chance of escape. And as the car drove down the drive, he heard in his mind his father's advice, the same given to all sons at this important time in their lives:

"Keep your mouth shut, your bowels open, and never volunteer."

As he looked out of the window with those august spectacles perched on the end of his nose, he suddenly saw the school fives court and behind that the cowsheds (why they had got that name he never knew) and the cricket field beyond. Surely that wasn't the geography of the place when he was there? And he took off the glasses and wiped his forehead. Looking out again, he saw the road … a small side road but nonetheless a road that wound round in front of the inn where they were staying. There was no fives court, no cowsheds, no cricket field. They had disappeared. Odd, he thought, and put the glasses on the table.

At the reception, most of the beaks that he had known were thankfully not there. They had either died, retired, or lapsed into such distinguished senility that it would be a pity to haul them back. So they mixed with the others and talked.

"Hello, Julian," a voice said, and he turned 'round to see the lanky figure of David Taplow. Unfortunately, David had changed little in appearance, and Julian felt decidedly jealous. He was as good-looking now as he was then. Julian wondered whether he was still as sadistic.

"Julia, may I introduce my old servitordux, David Taplow. David, this is Julia, my wife."

"Another one, Julian? You seem to be going through them rapidly!"
Julia flushed and Julian looked daggers at him.

"Still the same, I see, as diplomatic as ever. A servitordux, Julia, is an older boy, usually here in the sixth for whom you become a servant, for lack of a better word, while you are in the first two forms. You do what they say, at least within reason. Clean shoes, tidy their studies, make tea, open tins of sardines, carry billet-doux to other boys, etc."

"It's meant to build character," said David. "Shows what the other half must put up with. Carved up anyone I should know, recently?" he asked.

"No, and if I had I wouldn't tell you." Julian had become a rather distinguished surgeon in his afterlife, after leaving school, Oxford and St. Thomas's that is. He was a surgeon in ordinary to the Royal Household and last year received the customary knighthood, a KCVO. His wife was rather proud of being Lady Julia.

"Oh, and congrats on your K," David added and walked off.

"Not too pleasant," said Julia.

"No, he wasn't then, and he isn't now."

"But he's remarkably handsome."

"He was then, and he is now," said Julian wistfully.

"Ah, there you are, Sir Julian, and Lady Julia, too. How nice."

"Good evening, Bursar. Nice to see you again. Julia, this is Commander Blenkinsop, the bursar. He has been after us for cash, so that is how I know him. He's an old boy, but too young to have been here with me."

"Quite so, Sir Julian. Anyway, the headmaster and I are putting together a little do after this; would you and Lady Julia care to join us in the upper library?"

"No," said Julian.

After Blenkinsop had walked away, Julia asked him.

"How could you be so rude?"

"I only came here because you wanted to see it and them. Now that's done, can we go?"

"Not just yet. I want to stay for the dinner."

The dinner proceeded in its painful way. There were the speeches and the toasts, the forced laughter and the passing of the port (in the correct direction) and cigars. The wives looked a little out of place, but humored their husbands while they listened to all the reminiscences. Julia was seated next to one of the few friends that Julian had made while at Duster. Robert Probert had been a gentle boy who had grown into a gentle adult. He had been a superb pianist and organist at school and won an organ scholarship to the same Oxford college as Julian. They remained lifelong friends and both nurtured a somewhat bitter relationship with the school. Julia asked Robert for his reminiscences of her husband and was clearly engrossed.

"I had no idea I was so fascinating as a boy," he said to Julia as they walked out of Founder's court on a bitter January evening. The air was crisp and their breath condensed as they walked.

"You didn't wear those glasses I gave you," Julia said.

"No," he said, I left them back at the inn. "I forgot to bring them."

Back in their room with the radiators on full blast, Julian told his wife that he was going to have a bath. The bathroom was down the hall and at this time, unoccupied. He had been fortunate in not bumping into any Old Dorsetians during their stay. Not entirely by accident, as he had designed it so that they would have minimal interaction, coming back late, leaving early.

"I need a jolly good soak," he said.

"Take your time," Julia replied and settled into a comfortable, chintz-covered armchair, to read that part of the newspaper that she had not finished at breakfast. Perhaps it was the heat from the radiators, perhaps it was the long day, but her eyes felt tired and would not focus. I'll try those glasses, she thought, and rummaged around the room to find the gold pair in their exquisite gold case. 'I'm sure Julian won't mind if I borrow them,' she thought. She polished the lenses slowly, marveling at how they reflected the soft radiance of the light from the sconces, and then perched them on the bridge of her nose. Curious, she thought, where is that paper? I had it in my hand just now. And indeed, it was still there but had vanished from her view.

Instead, in front of her she saw a rather dingy room that was obviously a study of sorts. At a desk she saw a boy of about 17 who was bent over a book and clearly having some difficulty. After a short while, he got up and turned towards her. She recognized David Taplow as he must have been about 40 years before. She was so intrigued that it never occurred to her to question why all of this was unfolding in front of her. David ran to the door, opened it, and shouted out, "James, you lazy sod; I want you here now." There was a patter of running feet, and a breathless Julian James appeared at the door. Julia was astonished to see her husband as he must have looked at 14. He was slim, somewhat small for his age, with a mop of unruly auburn hair that he was constantly pushing back from his forehead.

"James," said David Taplow, "I need you to construe this. It's from *De Rerum Natura*. Lucretius. You're a bit of a Latin freak. What does this part mean? I've got to have this ready for tomorrow's period, and someone has taken the crib from the library."

"No, Taplow. Do your own work. I'm fed up with subbing for you. You're on your own this time."

Taplow turned to him, his green eyes angry and his pale cheeks flushed.

"What do you mean, you little …?"

"I mean what I say. I've had it with you. In fact, I've had it with everything."

"Shut up and translate it."

"No," said James defiantly.

Taplow got up and took Julian by his left arm, twisting it. Julian started to blubber with the pain.

"Stop it. Stop it. You're hurting me," he said ineffectually through his tears.

"You little shit," said Taplow, and twisting his arm further forced Julian towards the desk.

"Start writing," he commanded.

"I can't. You're twisting my arm."

"Write, damn you," said Taplow angrily, and he twisted it further. Suddenly, there was a snapping sound and a shrill shriek from Julian. The pain was more intense than anything he had ever felt. Julian collapsed onto the floor and lay there. He had passed out.

Alerted by the shrieking, Hodgson the housemaster came running up the stairs and threw open the door. Surveying the scene, he ordered the boys behind him who were gawping and rather enjoying what they saw: "Call Matron and you two lift him up and take him to my rooms. As for you Taplow, I think you have some explaining to do."

Julia took the glasses off and glanced at the paper she held in her left hand, the glasses in the right. She was aghast. Putting them on again, she saw a worried Taplow following Hodgson out of the room.

Taking the glasses off, she gently put them in their gold case, and opening a window she hurled them out into the night.

Julian came back looking radiant after his bath.

"Well, Julia, I was thinking that all in all, the day was not as awful as I thought it would be. If you want, we can stay for the rest of the festivities."

"No," said Julia. "I don't think I want to." There was compassion in the gaze that she gave her husband a slight break in her voice. "I think it's time for us to go home" she said softly.

He looked at her quizzically. After all, it had been at her insistence that they came, and now she wanted to leave early. And she was looking at him very strangely.

"Have you seen those glasses?" he asked.

"No," she said. "By the way, when we came back, I found this package in our room. It's addressed to you."

He opened it and in it was a book. There was a card attached and one word: "Sorry." The book was *De Rerum Natura*.

Chapter 4: Abyssinia

Jonathan Taplow, son of David, was late for choir practice at the Cathedral. He was a tall, lanky lad of 17, with soft curly blond hair and protruding upper teeth of which he was very conscious and slightly embarrassed. An alto, he had enjoyed singing since the age of 7 and was an excellent pianist and a passable organ player. He was cycling at a fast pace from his house in town.

As a scholar and in his final term in the upper sixth, he had the privilege of dossing out of college and was a resident in Gowers House, (housemaster Dr. Frederick Coates, the senior classics master). However, the presiding genius, or should it be genia (he pondered, never having been much of a Latinist), was his wife, Mrs. Coates ("Old Ma Coates" as she was known to generations of Dorsetians, and probably Henry VI himself!)

Jonathan, or "Spuds," as he was known to his friends, was well-liked for his affability; nothing ruffled him, and he was always available to lend a helping hand. His father had attended Duster but was expelled in his final year for some dark deed of which he never spoke. This hung as an accolade around Spuds' neck, the other boys in awe of someone with such distinguished parentage.

The wheels spun 'round furiously, and he was just able to stop in time, on the Old Inn Road, outside The Dorset Inn, to prevent himself from running over a shiny box in the middle of the way. He dismounted, adjusted his bicycle clips, and picked up the gleaming, golden object and put it in his pocket before setting off again. On reaching the cathedral, rehearsals for Evensong were in progress. Mr. Heathcote the choragus frowned as he entered. Slipping on his surplice,

Spuds took his place in the choir. But for some reason his soul wasn't in it, and he was aware of the mistakes that he was making as they wound their way through Tallis' Dorian Service. When they were finished, Mr. Heathcote came up to him.

"Well, Spuds, not up to your usual standards. You were a little off-key, especially in the Magnificat."

"Was I, Sir?" Spuds replied, knowing full well that he had been.

"Got a cold?"

"No, Sir."

"Something on your mind then?"

Spuds thought for a moment. He had known Heathcote for many years ever since coming to Duster, and they had a mutual respect and liking for each other. Normally, any form of trouble or difficulty should be discussed with the housemaster, and Dr. Coates was pleasant but rather an unworldly and remote character. Perhaps, Mrs. Coates?

Spuds deliberated as the rest of the choir bustled off back to school in anticipation of dinner.

"I think we'll have a cup of tea in the vestry," said Mr. Heathcote "Just a quick one, as I don't want you to be late for Hall."

"Yes, Sir," said Spuds.

"Well, Spuds, what is it? You haven't been yourself for a while now. I can see that. Do you want to tell me about it?"

Reluctantly, and suspecting that a trouble shared was a trouble doubled he said, "It's about medical school. Well, I'm not sure I want to go now."

"But you've been accepted and you're supposed to take up your place in October. As you know, these are fiercely fought over, as they are so limited. And St. Christopher's is a very prestigious institution. You should think yourself lucky."

"Yes, in a way I do. But I am beginning to have second thoughts."

"A bit late now, isn't it?"

And indeed, it was. For as long as he could remember, he had always wanted to be a doctor. Perhaps it was because he had seen so many of them as a young boy. His heart had been affected by some congenital condition and it was only just before he came to Duster that he could have the operation that all but cured it. He was much affected by his experience and wanted to be as kind to others as his medical team had been to him. And he was intrigued by the science, and this, truth be told, was his major pre-occupation. An outstanding biologist, chemist and mathematician — Physics never captured his imagination for some reason — a successful future was forecast. But now he was having serious second thoughts.

"I don't like dealing with gore, the seamy side of life, and all the emotional strain. Not to mention being up all night and expected to carry on all day as if one was as fresh as a daisy."

"My, my. What caused this revelation?" asked Heathcote.

"In the vac I stayed with Matthew Johnson and his father, who is a consultant at St. Christophers. He asked me what I thought life would be like."

"It isn't all chauffeurs and Harley Street consulting rooms you know," Dr. Johnson had said when he took Spuds and his son to St Christopher's one day. They followed him around the wards, to Casualty and to Outpatients. It was horrible, thought Spuds, who had turned green at the sight and smells. Finally, in a burst of genuine altruism, Dr. Johnson took them to the Clive Museum, one of the, if not *the*, leading pathology museums in the country. At the ground floor, Spuds was surrounded by oil paintings from the early nineteenth century of poor Chinese peasants whose tumours had grown to outlandish proportions. These were meant as instructive representations of what occurs when medical attention is a scarce resource, and had been painted by a medical missionary. This was followed by a trip to the obstetrics section where he was confronted by the ghastliest monstrosities. Dr. Johnson, who also was the museum director, relished showing the various jars to Spuds and Matthew, handing the most grotesque examples down for them to examine in closer detail.

The younger Johnson had been on this tour many times before, and he took a rather fiendish delight in the obvious effect it was having on Spuds. Finally, they went up to the fourth floor, which housed the Forensic Pathology section. For the best part of the century, St. Christopher's Hospital had provided the leading Home Office Pathologists, who had therefore been able to retain illustrative specimens for teaching purposes. One of these haunted Spuds for the next two weeks, to the extent that he had not been able to sleep.

It was the head of a red-haired man who had shot himself in the mouth with a rifle, at the outbreak of the second world war. His business had been threatened by the ensuing economic uncertainty and he had decided to take his own life. There was a thick opening running all the way from the top of the forehead to the chin, displacing one of the eyes. The accompanying card gave further details and pointed the student to observe that an apparent surface wound might occur because of the blast from a weapon discharged in a tight orifice.

"You shouldn't make a serious decision based on just one experience," said Mr. Heathcote.

"I felt so sick, sir. I'm sure I couldn't take it. I've just sent a letter to the senior tutor at St. Margaret's, Oxford to see whether the biology scholarship that they offered me was still open. If I applied again."

"Well, you're old enough to make up your own mind. Have you discussed this with your parents?"

"No, Sir, and I don't think that they would care very much. In fact, neither of them was particularly keen for me to go into medicine."

"I see. And have you talked about your experience with Dr. Johnson?"

"No, sir."

"Alright. It's really time for you to get to school, as you mustn't miss Hall. Goodbye, Taplow."

"Good bye, Sir. Abyssinia."

"What?"

"Abyssinia. I'll be seeing you."

"Oh, that. Off you go." And off he went.

It was later that day, back in his house in his bedroom, that he remembered the small case that he had picked up that afternoon. Examining it, he saw that it was a little dented. Looks like someone threw it out of a window, he thought. Opening the case gingerly, he saw a beautifully wrought pair of gold glasses. There was nothing really the trouble with Spuds' eyes. In fact, he was quite a passable bowler, although he had just missed being put into the first XI.

'I wonder what I would look like with glasses on,' he mused, placing them on the bridge of his nose as he regarded himself in the mirror above the washstand. A red-headed man stared back at him. Spuds involuntarily cried out with shock. He should have seen his own familiar reflection, protuberant teeth and all, but no, here staring at him was the red-headed man from the Clive Museum. Although the face was now intact, Spuds couldn't help remarking that the man was astonishingly ugly. The head that seemed to float on its own with no neck attached was talking to him.

"For God's sake, don't take any irreparable steps if you can avoid it. Don't you think I would like to have my life back?"

Spuds made no reply. He felt a heave come over him, and as he bent over the washstand, retching, the glasses fell off into the sink with a plonk. Alerted by the sounds, Matthew Johnson rushed in from his room next door.

"Whatever's the matter, Spuds?" he asked. And Spuds motioned to the mirror.

"Nothing to see there, except vomit. What's going on?"
Spuds was not inclined to talk and said that he had suddenly felt sick. Probably something he had eaten in Hall. The food was notoriously bad, and there were frequent outbreaks of gastric upset among the boys.

"Oh, well then. I'll get back to Lucretius. *De Rerum Natura*. A rather dry book, but my dad seemed to like it. Abyssinia."

"Abyssinia." Spuds picked up the glasses after washing them in the sink, put them carefully away in their case and threw them into the bottom of the cupboard.

A few days later after several worried nights and anxious days, he went to the cupboard to put on his Cricket togs. There was a match this afternoon, and he thought he might try a few practice shots in the nets before then. Pulling on his sweater, he heard a tinkling sound as the glasses case fell onto the wooden floor. He had tried not to think of them following the episode of a few days before, but he was fascinated despite the horror. He had resisted any temptation to try them on again, although he was strangely curious to see what other prophesies and ghastly sights might confront him. Rather like watching a venomous snake, he thought. Frightening and fascinating at the same time. 'I have a few minutes,' he said to himself, fumbling with the case. He put on the glasses. This time, the view was different. It was clearly a hospital ward, and the hospital was St. Christopher's. There were the usual groans and the hushed mumblings of conversations, the type that one has when one doesn't know how to comfort the dying. In the centre of his vision was a bed with curtains around it drawn. A nurse drew these back after a short time and he could see a clearly terminal Matthew Johnson in the bed. He had aged only slightly, so Spuds judged that this was not something that was in the distant future, if it would exist at all. Matthew looked very ill and frightened; his face was drawn and strikingly pale, and there was a drip in his left arm. He was talking to a man whose back was towards Spuds. They seemed to be engrossed in an earnest conversation. Then the view changed, and there was a close-up of the white-coated man as he turned. With a shudder, Spuds saw himself.

"I'm so glad you told me," said Matthew. "Although I sensed it already. Dad couldn't tell me, and I know that he thought it would be best coming from you. We've always been close you and I, haven't we?"

"Yes," said Spuds, "very."

"That bloody treatment didn't work, did it?"

"No."

"Is there anything else?"

"No."

"So that's it?

"That's it," Spuds said and looked away. There was a pause during which neither spoke.

"How do you like medical school, Spuds? Dad told me that you are doing very well."

Spuds was embarrassed. "It's alright," he said.

"I'm so glad that you're here. You can come often and be with me when …"

"Yes, I'll be here. Abyssinia."

"Abyssinia," replied Matthew sadly, and Spuds left.

The glasses steamed up and Spuds took them off. He lapsed into a chair. Then after looking at his watch, he ran his hands through his hair. He subconsciously put the glasses in his pocket and getting up stiffly made off for the cricket nets. On the way down, he tripped over a partially hidden boulder and the glasses in their case fell out of his pocket. And there they lay until a short while later the groundsman drove his steamroller over them, fracturing the glasses into a mess of shards and twisted metal. The sounds of clapping from the cricket pitch was just enough to cover the protesting groan that seemed to come from the glasses as they shattered.

Part IV: College Bound

Grace, is said before and after meals at St Margaret's College, Oxford. Extracts have been used as the focus of each of the following stories.

Chapter 1: Benedictus, Benedicat
(May he who is blessed provide blessings
to others)

The chapel of St. Margaret's College in the University of Oxford is a mediaeval structure and therefore appropriately gloomy and dark. Formerly the parish church of St. Andrew, it had been reorganized as the college chapel in the thirteenth century and expanded to a size where it was larger than the cathedral in that city. The Major contemplated this as he was being led around the structure, built to the glory of God and the greater glory of the founder of the college, a certain bishop now long forgotten except in the benefactor's prayer — an obligatory addendum to each and every service held in the building. His cousin by marriage, the primus (or college head) was showing Major Sir John Cylburn around.

"And this, John, is one of our most famous monuments, the memorial to Sir Matthias Birdstone, the founder of the Birdstone Fellowships and a major college benefactor," said the primus, Lord Hinchbury.

The Major looked at the Elizabethan monument and shuddered. He was unable to separate whether the cold of the building or the sadness of the inscription made him respond that way.

"Of course, John, you must have been in here during your time at Cardinal, just down the road from here."

"No, Lord Hinchbury, I can't say that I have."

As the primus droned on about the Wren screen and so on, the Major's mind wandered to the day two months ago when his wife had spoken the fateful words at breakfast: "You know, John, you need a job."

The Major looked at his wife in surprise and with the buttered and marmaladed toast sticking halfway out of his mouth said, "What? Why?"

"John, don't speak with your mouth full. You are spraying the table with crumbs."

"But Mary …"

Lady Mary continued: "Since Nicholas' death you have not been the same. And you should have got over that by now. It's nearly five years."

The Major put the remains of the toast down delicately onto the plate in front of him and stared at it. The death of his nephew had been an event from which he had prayed desperately to be spared the feeling of guilt and loss. The boy had died during the war, but not in it. That was the cruelty of the thing. He was going to enlist in the Navy and John had been asked by Nicholas' mother (Mary's sister) to talk him out of it over lunch. And on the way out of the club, the boy had been run over. He pushed the Major out of the way of a speeding vehicle and sacrificed himself. John could never understand why fate, or God, had allowed this. But while neither quite religious nor spiritual, yet he prayed for release from the torture of spirit.

"I have spoken to my cousin, David Hinchbury, and he would like to talk to you about a position at the college," Mary said.

"But I don't want to. Really, I don't. I'm quite alright as it is. Also, I don't want an academic appointment, and I don't have the right background anyway."

"John, you spend your time moping around the house and grounds, chatting to the gardeners and aimlessly calling on the tenants for tea. You don't have a purpose. And you need one."

John considered this very carefully. As always, his wife was right, and he knew it.

"But …"

"But me no buts! As Shakespeare, I think, said. It is settled. I've bought you a train ticket and David will see you the day after tomorrow in the chapel of St. Margaret's at ten. Don't forget that he is a stickler for punctuality."

And so John found himself, with wandering mind, listening to his wife's cousin talking endlessly about the glory of the college's unique architecture. He mused that the gloominess of the surroundings was so appropriate; it matched his own disposition.

"And now that is quite enough of that," said Lord Hinchbury, and the Major agreed silently while trying to look suitably attentive. "Let's go back to my lodgings. I have a few things I want to talk to you about."

The Major followed the primus out of the chapel and into St. Margaret Street, to the forbidding Edwardian structure that was the Primus's lodgings, known to all Old Chasians (as old members were called), as 'Wren,' but why no one could remember or, for that matter, cared.

"Hello, Major," said Joan, the primus' wife after the primus introduced them and then gave drinks. A good sherry before lunch at the lodgings. Not in college this time.

"I know that you must feel very bad about Nicholas," said Lady Hinchbury. "But you simply can't blame yourself. These things happen - uncalled for and unexpectedly. That's why they are called accidents." The Major wondered whether his wife and Joan had been having an earnest chat on the telephone prior to his arrival. Priming the primus, he thought wryly and looked down at the table.

"Accident or act of God," he said. "I've been spared in two world wars, shrapnel in the first but still alive, damn it."

"You mustn't speak that way. It's unfair and ungenerous," said Joan.

"Why isn't there mandatory death at say 60 or even 40? Let the young survive and learn their own lessons so that they don't repeat ours. Why is it that the young have to die?" said the Major bitterly. "I've seen too much of it and Nicholas' death was the last straw."

There was a silence. Lord Hinchbury got up, walked to the sideboard, returned with a bottle of claret and poured a third glass for the Major and a first for himself and his wife. "I'm 60 this year, and not quite ready to die yet," he said with a laugh. "Besides, I know that you have made Mary very happy. And I think that that is a reason for your existence."

"Perhaps," said the Major, not quite convinced.

"Well, now to business. I have a vacancy for a bursar. Our old one, General Mason-Jones, retired and I need someone with a good calculating brain to take over. You had an excellent degree in Maths schools, I believe, and spent a good deal of your youth ..."

"Yes, yes, I know. Playing cards as a living. Yes, I have a good memory and can also do calculations in my mind. That's how I survived for many years. But not now. Not since Mary."

"But you don't have to play cards as bursar. Manage the daily accounts, contract with contractors, keep the Fellows' expenses in order, and the college cellar and kitchen. Oh, and there is one other thing."

"Yes?"

"Yes. I need someone who can interact with donors, Old Chasians, and people like that. You know, press the flesh and caress the wallet. That sort of thing. I'm hopeless at that," he said as his wife nodded in agreement.

"You want me to pimp for the college, is that it?"
Lord and Lady Hinchbury looked shocked.

"I withdraw that uncalled-for comment," said the Major, embarrassed by his outburst.

"I know that you have been under some strain, and of course allowances must be made," said the primus, primly. And looking at the Major's tie, he noted the red cardinal's hats that adorned it, which resembled flying saucers. "Of course, you're not an Old Chasian, so I can't expect you to feel the same way about this college as you might for, let us say, your school or college or even your regiment."

The Major felt nothing for any of them.

"Thank you, Lord Hinchbury for an excellent morning, and you Lady Hinchbury for an excellent lunch. But I must be getting back." And the Major rose from the mahogany table.

"Will you consider the position? I really would appreciate your help," said the primus.

"I'll consider it," he said, and was helped on with his hat and coat, and in a rather sour mood he tramped his way back to Oxford station.

****

128

"You look most distinguished and very smart," said the Major's wife a few months later as she helped him on with his brand-new MA gown, the symbol of his status. Lady Mary had been persuasive to the point of being insistent on the matter, and now here they were in a small, comfortable, albeit drafty, house on Holywell Street. Their own home was in a neighbouring county and only about 30 miles distant so at a stretch they might have lived there, too. But they could have the best of both worlds if they took up the college's offer of accommodation and later decide how to divide their time. Their factor was doing an excellent job managing the estate, albeit under very difficult circumstances. Taxation and inflation had affected both ends of the deal, firstly by eroding the profitability of farming and second by heavily taxing any profits. The Major had shrugged. "At least we have the salary of the bursary," he said to his wife. "All 300 pounds per annum!"

"Now be nice in Hall, and don't lose your temper with the dons," said his wife, as she recalled her own time as an undergraduate at Somerville. "You know they have a cloistered life and can be a little, how shall I say, sarcastically inbred in their humour." The Major nodded and left.

In the Hall, which was long and almost as gloomy as the chapel, the Fellows, collectively known as the high table due to their location in the room, marched in led by the primus. There was the gentle swishing of gowns as the undergraduates stood up as one from the benches on which they, most uncomfortably, sat. Grace was said by the senior Birdstone Scholar (termed "Berson" in college speak) in attendance and then all sat down. The undergraduates were clearly in a good mood that evening, and the Hall reverberated to loud conversation and laughter. At the high table, the Major was seated next to the primus, and to his right was a man in a loud check suit and college tie. The primus had made the table arrangements carefully. The 'gentleman' on the Major's right, a Mr. St. John DeVere was a prospective benefactor, a man of considerable wealth and the owner of a large chain of betting shops throughout the country.

"Well, Major, or Sir John," said DeVere, "Wot should I call you? Not used to all these posh terms and so on."

"Oh, why not 'bursar'? 'Bursar' will do nicely."

"Well, the college is after my dosh, and I want to give them a bunch. Except wot I want to give my son."

"Your son?"

"Yes. He's coming up next term. Just finished at Dorchester School, you know. I'm very proud of him. Not that his mum and I had any schooling. Why in my day, our parents couldn't afford any education. Our education was selling crap from the barrow in Bermondsey market."

"You're very fortunate," said the Major.

"You taking the mick, are you?" said DeVere with some anger in his voice.

"Not at all. I'm just saying that what you imagine and the reality are often different."

"Oh. Well, I think my life would be different if I'd had a posh education like you."

"Perhaps. And perhaps not," said the Major laconically. And they returned to silence.

"What odd cutlery," said DeVere looking at the setting in front of him. "You'd think a posh place like this would have everything matching, wouldn't you? First thing I'll do is give them money to buy some proper stuff. Asprey's or Garrards. And then those awful pictures," he said as he surveyed the dour expressions on the faces of significant old Chasians that adorned the walls and glared at the undergraduates as a warning.

"Wot you need here is a nice row of landscapes, and a nude or two. That'll cheer the boys up no end, that will," and he gave a coarse laugh that subsided into a fit of loud and prolonged coughing. The conversation in Hall stopped, but resumed again when the fit subsided with a loud but partially stifled belch.

"Sconce," shouted a young voice from the Hall.

"Wot!" exclaimed DeVere.

"You'll see," said the Major as an auburn-haired boy with forelock falling down his forehead approached the primus and handed him a note.

"Placet?" he asked diffidently.

"Placeo," replied the primus and the boy walked back to his place. The primus rapped on the table with his gavel and a college servant appeared with a two-pint, silver double-handled bowl that he gave to the boy sitting next to the one who had just come to high table. He rose, and taking the bowl by the handles proceeded to drink.

"It's a sconce. You can only ask for it if you are senior to the boy who is sconced. He's sconced for either talking shop, or religion, or mentioning Keble college, or badly of a girl. The sconcee has to drink two pints of college beer in one go or has to pay for it. Otherwise, it's the sconcer's responsibility."

"I like traditions like that," said DeVere. "And so will my boy when he comes up."

"I wonder," mused the Major. "By the way, is that a college tie you're wearing?"

"Yes," said DeVere, "and with the cash I'm giving the college, it's not a cheap buy."

The Major shrugged and attacked the dry pudding with a spoon but without success.

After Hall, liqueurs and coffee were served in the SCR, the senior common room. The candlelight reflecting off the dark oak, Tudor linen-pleat panelling created a mellow atmosphere, and the senior Fellows who attended were lulled into a torpor that contrasted with their usually rancorous relationships among one another. The primus was doing the rounds introducing Mr. DeVere to the distinguished group, and the Major from a distance observed the amused expressions on their faces after each introduction was made and the pair had moved on to assault another don.

After all had left to either go back to their digs in college or their wives, Lord Hinchbury asked Mr. DeVere and the Major to stay behind for a moment.

"Mr. DeVere, we are certainly honoured to have you here this evening. Thank you for coming. Shall you be staying in college tonight or going back to town?"

"My pleasure, I'm sure," said DeVere. "And my choffer is outside and will drive me back.

The primus looked awkward and nudged the Major in the ribs. "Say something," he hissed and responded to the querying look on the Major's face. "Anything?"

"Mr. DeVere, when might we have the pleasure of your company again?" asked the Major weakly.

"Oh, you mean so that you can seal the deal? See whether you get it now or later? The quick and the dead," DeVere chuckled, and the Major was somewhat surprised at the liturgical quote.

"No, not at all," shot the Major.

"But, of course we should be most grateful for ..." and the primus stopped.

"Well, gents, I'll tell you. I've had a good time. Great time. And I am looking forward to more such when my boy, Tom, comes here next term. And I'm used to paying for my fun. Always have and fair's fair. But what you want is a lot. And I want something in return. That's how people like me were brought up. No handshakes and old boys' honour. Just simple: I give you something and you give me something." The Major and the primus looked at each other and were clearly a trifle uncomfortable.

"I'm sure that something can be arranged ... For example ..." started the primus.

"Lord Hinchbury, that's not good enough. It's not what you might dole out to me and expect me to be thankful and go on my way. No. It's wot I want. And I always get what I want."

The primus paled and the Major stifled a chuckle. He knew where this was going.

"Of course, within reason and ..." the primus blustered.

"How can we help?" asked the Major in a conciliatory voice.

"I want to give you new knives and forks to replace the second-hand rubbish you use. I want to get rid of those pictures and give you some nice ones. Brighten up the Hall, it will. And I want fluorescent lighting in the Hall and chapel so that the boys can see wot they're eating and where they're going. And I want a memorial in chapel. A large one. Next to that Birdshit geezer."

The primus was stunned. "We all thought a plaque in chapel, or a portrait, small of course, in the JCR perhaps ...?" said the primus.

"Nah! A fellowship at the least. And not honorary. I can teach the boys something, I can. Something about life. Not about Beowulf or calculus. Oh yes, I know a little bit about wot you lot do up here. My boy, Tom, talks to me about it. Loves me he does, in spite of my rough ways. He'll be a gentleman, he will. Not like his dad. And he'll have so

132

much cash that he won't know wot to do with it, he will. And so will you, if …"

"Well," said the primus, "I'm afraid it's getting rather late for all of us," and he gave the Major a significant glance. "The bursar will see you to the lodge." And the bursar did and returned to the SCR as instructed afterwards.

"The man's impossible," said Lord Hinchbury. "Any suggestions?"

"Not really."

"Well, I can't pretend we don't want the money. We don't really need it. But …"

"But you would like to be remembered as the primus who brought in the largest benefaction since Sir Mathias Birdshit."

"You're being very cynical this evening, Bursar," and the Major noted the disapproval in the primus's voice.

"I really love this college. I went here as a boy and have stayed ever since. It's my life. Don't you have anything you care for? Or did the war make you into a cynical skeleton wandering about aimlessly in a Savile Row suit? No feelings, no imagination, just waiting to die. To join the others who died when you didn't? Guilt. Unfulfilled. Sterile."

The Major thought of Nicholas and of his own friends who had died in front of him, and of his own suffering in both wars. And the loss. And above it all, the love, the deep love, the strongest emotion of all, that he had for his wife.

"I'll see what I can do, Sir," he said softly and walked out into the night.

****

The man at the other end of the line took a long time to answer. "Where the hell can he be?" queried the major as he tapped his finger against the wall in front of him. Still the ringing and still no answer. He was about to put the phone down when he heard the customary click, and then a pause.

"Pettibone here. Who is this?"

133

"Hello, Pettibone. How are you?" There was a pause at the other end, while Pettibone clearly was trying to place the voice indistinct due to the poor quality of the long-distance line.

"Pettibone, it's Cylburn."

"Oh, you don't have to tell me, Major. How could I forget? How are things? How's the missus?"

"Yes, yes. Quite. How's the business?" replied the Major impatiently.

"First class, absolutely first class," Mr. Pettibone lied. "Can't complain, and if I did who would care anyway. Got to look on the bright side."

"Look, Pettibone. I'm in a spot of bother. Or rather not me, a friend, actually a relative of my wife's."

"Prison then, is it?"

"No, nothing like that. Nothing like that at all."

"What then?"

"Look, I don't want to talk about it on the phone. Come to the club; you know the one in St. James, and we'll talk about it there."

"Over lunch?"

"Over lunch."

"Say one o'clock today?"

"Today? Well, Major that's rather short notice and I'm rather …" Mr. Pettibone wanted to sound busy and employed even if he was not.

"Please. You would be doing me a great favour." And Pettibone agreed to go, remembering the great wrong he had done the Major in the past. Yes, he had gone to prison for it. Eventually. After he had confessed. Eventually. The Major had appreciated his courage, but Mr. Pettibone was never sure whether or not the Major had completely forgiven him. And because of that, he would do anything for the Major. Anything at all.

"Will he see you?" asked Lady Mary.

"Yes," said the Major with relief.

At the club, Mr. Pettibone seemed not quite his cheerful self. He wasn't always comfortable in unfamiliar surroundings, although he had been here before on one or two occasions with the Major. He found the environment somewhat claustrophobic, and the shabby furniture reminded him of an unsuccessful antique shop. He cast an appraising eye over the paintings and trappings. As a dealer himself (Pettibone, Sons and Langford, Dealers and Valuers of Fine Antiques), his trained gaze told him that there was nothing here of consequence. Just like himself, he thought; and perhaps some of the members too, although of that he could not be sure.

The Major was in good spirits and guided him to the table. The candle in its long-stemmed holder was lit to show occupancy and the meal began.

"How's the missus, Major?"

"Very well. Very well indeed, thank you. She sends her regards. We should have you over. In fact, I would like to talk to you about that."

"Oh, yes?" asked Mr. Pettibone warily.

"Ronald, please get Mr. Pettibone another pint of Bass," called the Major.

"I have taken a job," continued the Major, "and I have to confess that this wasn't my idea; it was my wife's."

"Yes, I was sorry to hear about your nephew. It was in the papers. Five years ago, wasn't it? Need something to occupy your mind, you do."

The Major marveled at Mr. Pettibone's perspicacity. He always seemed to be able to get straight to the bottom of things.

"You certainly understand me. Or is it human nature in general? Yes, Mary insisted that I needed to do something to get over it. Get out of the house. I don't know whether it was for her sanity or mine."

"Were you close?"

"Not really. In fact, I had only met Nick, er, Nicholas for the first time that day. We had lunch. Here at the club. At this table."

And Mr. Pettibone shuddered. He wasn't superstitious, but he made a note of not drinking too much. Had to keep his wits about him when crossing St, James Square, clearly. Never know whether he might be run over by a perambulator or worse, an ambulance.

"He didn't like to be called Nick," added the Major as his mind wandered back.

"No point dwelling on it," said Mr. Pettibone gently.

135

"No. No, of course not. Of course not …" and the Major looked away so that Pettibone couldn't see the anguish in his face. Or the tearing of his eye.

"So, I now work at a college in Oxford. I'm the bursar there."

"Yes?" replied Pettibone wondering what all of this had to do with him.

"I look after the college finances and so on."

"And you want me to check the accounts. Cook stealing from the kitchen? Or one of them professors with a clever hand in the till?"

"No, nothing like that. It's about a benefactor, a donor. Frankly, it will mean a lot to the college if he gives them the money, and it is a lot. And I don't know how to manage it."

"And you think I do?" asked Mr. Pettibone incredulously. "What could I have in common with someone like that?"

The Major latched on to the word "common" and then shook it away.

"The person in question has … a different perspective on life. The primus — the head of the college — told me that I need to handle it, and a great deal may depend on it."

"Like what?"

"New accommodation, new wiring, new library, new everything actually. I am sure that the boys would like a toilet, or a bath provided."

"So where do I come in?"

"I need you to talk to him. I think that you both speak the same language, as it were."

"Oh, ho! I see. You mean the common touch. I gather that he isn't out of the top drawer then?"

"If you choose to put it that way, Mr. Pettibone," and the Major wondered why he had never asked what Mr. Pettibone's first name was.

"I do choose to put it that way. And Major, I am surprised at you. You want me to do your dirty work because you think that he is common and I am common and we have that in common?"

The conversation was not going at all the way that the Major had planned. He had hoped that Mr. Pettibone would look at this as another adventure. Or possibly a puzzle to be solved using his excellent interpersonal skills.

"Look here, Pettibone; I understand that it appears that way. But from another perspective, let's say you had invited a Russian to dinner, a Russian who didn't speak English. Wouldn't it be kind to have someone there who spoke the same language, who understood his culture, knew where he was coming from? Wouldn't that be a kindness?"

"P'raps," said Mr. Pettibone, still somewhat put out.

"And the college would also appreciate your assessment of one or two items: a painting and some furniture that they were interested in putting up for sale. The primus specifically asked whether you would give the college an opinion and possibly handle the sale. That is if you have the time," the Major lied.

Mr. Pettibone was never immune to a call to his vanity or his pocket. Especially if he could make a good amount out of it. And this had possibilities, decided possibilities.

"Asked for me specifically, did he?"

"Definitely."

"Let me think it over, Major. Let me sleep on it."

There was a pause and then Pettibone said, "What's the chap's name, if I dare ask?"

"I don't see any point in hiding it. It's a Mr. DeVere."

"St. John DeVere?" Mr. Pettibone could not refrain from a soft whistle.

"Why, do you know him, Pettibone?"

"Er, no. Well, yes. Well, no. No, I don't. I know the name, of course. Big on the betting circuit. Horseracing, gee-gees, you know. Owns a string of betting shops. Done well for hisself, hasn't he? Out of horses I mean."

"You could say that."

"I just did." And Mr. Pettibone drank the last of his beer and muttered abstractedly into his glass. "Well, well. That's first class, absolutely first class."

And walking carefully across the road to avoid the traffic, Mr. Pettibone made up his mind.

****

137

"I'm very much looking forward to seeing that Mr. Pettibone of yours," said Lady Mary.

"You won't be rough on him will you, Mary?" asked the Major.

"I would really like to give him a piece of my mind. That was a nasty thing he did on the Queen Mary, planting those counterfeit notes and the stolen necklace on you so that he could get away."

"But he did confess."

"Yes, eventually. But you must have had a terrible time until he did."

"It's water under the bridge," said the Major. "I think he thought it a wheeze, a prank,"

"Well, I don't think it's very funny at all.".

"Please don't be harsh. You'll like him, you'll see. I do."

"Why?"

"Because he has a naturalness about him. He's ..." The Major was grasping for the words to describe Mr. Pettibone.

"Don't say he's honest, because ..."

"I was going to say, he's down to earth."

"So is the head gardener and you don't particularly like him." Lady Mary was rather pleased with that retort.

"Mr. Clark? No, I don't. He used to twist my ears when I was a kid. He must be 80 if he's a day. Where is the blighter?" The Major looked at his watch. We'll be late for Hall if he doesn't come soon.

"Are you sure that David knows exactly what you're up to? With Pettibone, DeVere, and all that, I mean?"

"Yes, I'm sure he knows. Quite certain," said the Major uncertainly.

A short while later, the Major opened the door to a knock. Mr. Pettibone was there on the doorstep in his dinner jacket.

"Aren't you going to let me in, Major?" he asked. The Major looked back at the hallway clock. "Yes, we have five minutes or so, and then we'll have to walk over."

"Mary, I'd like you to meet Mr. Pettibone," the Major nervously said.

"Oh," said the Major's wife with a forced smile, "so you're the famous Mr. Pettibone. I've heard a lot about you."

"Pleased to meet you, my Lady," said Mr. Pettibone noting the frost in Mary's tone. "Chilly for this time of year isn't it, Madame?"

"Is it? I hadn't noticed. Hadn't you better take Mr. Pettibone over, John? It must be getting late." And she helped the Major on with his gown over his military mess dress uniform and medal miniatures. She handed him his hood.

"What's that red thing? asked Pettibone. Is it a scarf?"

"No, it's called a hood. Some of us call it a nosebag. It shows your degree. This is an MA, a Master of Arts."

"Cor!" said Mr. Pettibone.

They walked over in silence. On reaching the college gate, Mr. Pettibone stopped and turned to the Major. "So will Reggie, I mean Mr. DeVere, be here tonight?"

"Yes. That's why you're here, remember? Reggie?"

"Sorry. Was thinking of someone else completely. Someone I used to know. Had a similar name. Can't quite remember it. Knew him from the gee-gees and well before that too. Heard something about him from an old friend recently," Mr. Pettibone blustered, and then was silent. Thinking.

The college porter came forward and addressed the Major and Mr. Pettibone with that supercilious obsequiousness that is a particularity of the species.

"Primus' complements, Sir John. But as you're late, you're to go straight to Hall and wait there."

"In the dog house are we?" asked Pettibone.

"Shut up, Pettibone," said the Major none too kindly. The evening had not started well. He was disturbed that his wife didn't like Pettibone, but then if he were in her shoes, perhaps he wouldn't either. It's different if you're a man, he thought. Besides, he would take Pettibone back later, and then he could work his charm on Mary.

They walked up the stairs to the back of the Hall, where there was a small anteroom. A candelabrum on the table cast a light over a gleaming cut glass decanter and Mr. Pettibone walked up to it.

"First class," he said, rubbing his hands together. "Just the thing to steady the nerves." And he was about to pour himself a drink when the sound of several footsteps approaching caused him to put the decanter down again.

"Pettibone, just a word before they arrive," said the Major. "Don't drink or start eating before grace and before the primus sits. It's a college custom." And at that, the door opened and the primus, fellows and guests came in.

"Good evening, Bursar. We missed you at sherry," said the primus, none too pleased.

"Sorry, Primus. I lost my miniatures and couldn't find them for a while. I had to keep Mr. Pettibone waiting too," he lied, and thought to himself, "If I continue on this path, my nose will be so long I could dig a trench with it."

"Mess dress tonight, then?"

"Yes, I thought that it might be a change."

"Expecting a battle, are we?" asked the senior tutor. "Surprised you didn't bring your service revolver."

"Primus, may I introduce Mr. Pettibone? Gentlemen."

The dons bowed slightly and wondered where on earth the bursar could have found such a character. As they shuffled in and the boys in Hall rose, the primus took the Major aside and whispered, "Make sure he sits next to DeVere."

As they took their seats, the Major noticed a particular look on DeVere's face.

"Hello, Reggie," said Mr. Pettibone, "fancy seeing you here."
Mr. DeVere said nothing.

"You've gone up in the world," Mr. Pettibone added.

"Don't know what you're talking about. Do I know you? asked DeVere.

"Oh, yes, Reggie. Yes indeed. We're old friends. From the Scrubs. Years ago, when you were doing time for … what was it? Robbery with violence? I never forget a face, Reggie. Even after plastic surgery. It's the eyes, Can't disguise the eyes. Still, the docs did a good job on you"

DeVere took a deep breath in. "Look, I don't want any trouble. Not here. Not now. Suppose I do know you. So then what?"

The Major was straining to hear the conversation being carried on in hushed tones. And the primus, on his left, was giving him all manner of instructions about the handling of Mr. DeVere:

"Don't upset him, John. People like that can be very sensitive you know."

140

"I know. I just hope to God that Pettibone knows it, too." replied the Major, and there was a different meaning in his words. Clearly, DeVere and Pettibone had met before and although he could not hear everything that was being said, the general tone and the body language did not bode well.

"Look, Bert, I am trying to do good here. My boy is coming up next term. I want to smooth things for him. Give him things I never had. And I like tradition. I like history. Never had roots, and now's my chance."

"Balls," said Mr. Pettibone. "All you want is money, and now you want some prestige. And whitewash."

"No, I've changed. We can. My wife … well when she was dying, she asked me to pledge to reform. For the boy's sake, for her memory's sake. I done her a lot of wrong in my life, but I loved her, and she, poor cow, well she loved me. She loved me to death. So, I can't refuse, can I?"

"Bullshit, Reggie. You were a crook and you're still a crook. You can't change. You wouldn't know how to. And after that last bank job, well off you went and ditched the others. Turned against them, got a good QC, bribed the police and kept the money. Then disappeared. And now here you are with a new face, a new identity. You think you can put everything right by giving cash to a college. Hope to wipe all of that out. Well, I've news for you. You will be in all the papers if you're not already. Them friends of yours, them in the clink, they have contacts, Reggie. You're not out of the woods. You never were. They're biding their time. And where better to get at you than when you least expect it. An Oxford college full of old women dons who would scream and run for cover if a starting pistol was fired in the air above their heads! No, Reggie, you're done for. And I ain't coming to the funeral."

Mr. DeVere looked visibly shaken. The primus, thinking things must be going well, leaned over the Major and asked Mr. DeVere whether he needed anything. He did not answer.

"Look, Reggie," continued Mr. Pettibone. I'll make it easy for you. I won't tell them about you and where the cash came from, and you go home after tonight and we don't want to hear another word from you again."

"But Tom's coming up. I can't not visit him."

141

"Oh, yes you can. And you will. We don't want you here, Reggie. Not your sort."

"But they were all crooks, weren't they? That Sir Matthews Birdshit who's such a big deal here. Didn't he screw a lot of orphans and widows out of their savings, then put the cash into a license to print bibles and leave all his dosh to this place to save his soul?"

"I don't know, and I don't care. That is all history. We are talking about now. And I don't want any of my friends connected with you."

"Friends, Bert. Friends! What friends could you have here? Who?"

Mr. Pettibone knew who his friend was, but he did not deign to grant an answer.

"If you come back here, and if you give them any of your stolen money, I will tell them about you and who you really are. What you've done. And it will be in the papers. With your picture. And all that expensive plastic surgery won't save you. If I recognized you, so will they. I recognized you last year at the races. And now Reginald Gall the bank robber who disappeared has been found. In Oxford. And his name's DeVere. And the police want to find him; and so do his old messmates in Wormwood Scrubs, and the family of the man you killed after the robbery. Strange name he had, didn't he? Like Gander. 'Goosey, goosey gander whither do you wander?'" And he sang that old nursery rhyme softly into DeVere's ear.

There was a pause and the primus got up and withdrew his chair and stood behind it. The entire hall stood up. He rapped the gavel on the table and there was complete silence.

"*Benedictus, benedicat,*" he said.

"What?" asked DeVere, and the don on his right said, "Mr. DeVere. This college has the longest grace before meals, and the shortest after.

"But what does it mean?"

"It means: Let he who is blessed, bless others with good deeds."

"Oh," said DeVere.

As they walked out, the primus stayed to join the Major, Mr. Pettibone, and DeVere.

"I hope you will join us for port and desert in the SCR, Mr. DeVere? Oh, and you too, Mr. Pettibone."

"The SCR?" asked DeVere.

"Yes, the Senior Common Room, sort of our parlour. Where we sit and chat and all that. "

Mr. Pettibone gave DeVere a sharp glance, and then said, "Mr. DeVere told me that he wasn't feeling well, so he would like to stay here until tomorrow if that's okay with you, Sir." He planned to have a further word with DeVere later that evening.

"Of course. Steward," the primus said, "go and tell Gandivance to prepare the Queen's Room for Mr. DeVere."

"Yes, Sir," said the steward, whose distinguishing feature was his enormous feet. So large were they that all the boys of the college took bets to estimate their size and to guess when he would next trip going up the steps to the Hall. No one had won so far.

"Yes, Sir."

"Gandivance, did you say?" asked Mr. DeVere.

"Yes, odd name, isn't it?"

"I knew a Gandivance. Is he an old man?"

"No, quite young I should say," the primus replied.

Going across the front quad over the cobblestones towards the Queen's Room, the Major turned to Mr. DeVere and asked, "That was an odd name. I wonder whether it's Cornish?"

"No, no it's not," said DeVere. "It's from Bristol."

"How in heaven's name do you know?"

"I told you; I knew a Gandivance once."

"Knew?" asked the Major. "Why, is he dead?"

Mr. DeVere paled but did not answer. Looking at the ground, he slowly walked across the quad almost bumping into a young man coming in the opposite direction.

"Oh, there you are, Gandivance," said the primus. "Fixed the heater, have you?"

"Yes, Sir. I fixed it alright," said the young man and walked away whistling a popular air.

"Well, goodnight, Bursar, and Mr. Pettibone. Let's have breakfast tomorrow and get Mr. DeVere to join us. I hope that your conversation was satisfactory."

"Oh, yes, Sir. I think it was," said Mr. Pettibone.

****

The night was cold. The college was even colder. The primus hoped to provide central heating, at the very least to the don's accommodation, with the money that DeVere was going to give the college. But the thought of fluorescent light in Hall, and nudes on the wall there? He shuddered, and not from the nip in the air.

In the Queen's Room, DeVere was pacing up and down. For some years he had tried to lead a respectable life, or at least as respectable a life as a bookmaker can lead. And despite his past. His very degenerate past. Yes, he still wasn't entirely on the up and up, but he had tried to do his best. He had been philanthropic, given to good causes, sent large sums anonymously to the Gandivance's at Christmas. He had done his bit. But what if that old fraud Pettibone was right? What if there were people here who knew about him? Who recognized him? Strange about that man, Gandivance. College electrician. Had he overheard the conversation with Pettibone? Was he serving dinner, helping out that night in hall? Well, he would have to find out tomorrow. Anyway, it was too late now, and he had foolishly allowed Pettibone to maneuver him into staying in college. My, what a gloomy place. He wondered whether Tom would stick it for the full four years. Of course, Tom didn't need to stay in college. He could have rooms at the Randolph if he liked. Or they could fix up his rooms in college.

He looked at the four-poster bed and said out loud, "I wonder whether Elizabeth I slept in it. She done a lot of sleeping around, that gal did. A regular scrubber I think." And he walked over to the thick oak door and locked it with the key he had been given. Then as an afterthought, he slid a large and heavy chest of drawers over to block it. He inspected the windows. "Thick them are, and locked." He was satisfied that no one would be able to get in, at least not that night. "And," he thought, "if anyone tries it on during the day ..." and from the breast pocket of his dinner jacket, he drew a large Smith and Wesson .45 and opening the breech checked it. "All righty righty," he said.

There was a knock on the door.

144

"Reggie, open up."

No response.

"Open up. I need to talk to you. It's about … Gandivance."

DeVere did not reply.

Further knocking.

"Have it your own way, Reggie," said Mr. Pettibone and shuffled off.

Despite the cold, the exertion of moving the chest of drawers and Mr. Pettibone's words had made him sweat.

"Wot I need is a bath," and he opened the door to the bathroom and noted with satisfaction the large bathtub. He turned on the taps, humming softly to himself. "Goosey, goosey gander whither do you wander."

The floor was brick and there was a draft. He had goosebumps. Taking off his underpants, he slid into the warm bath and submerged as much of himself as he could. He lay there thinking. He was thinking of his wife. What would she have said about it all? Would she be impressed that he was here with all those educated people, and they were eating out of his hand? He doubted it. She had been too down-to-earth, too level-headed to be impressed by such trivia. What mattered were people, what they were, not who they were. But she would be pleased with Tom. The apple of her eye, that boy was, and of his, too. Only problem was that the boy was soft. He needed to learn the hard lessons of life. But then, he would have so much money that none of that mattered.

What was that sound? He realized that his teeth were chattering and that the bath water was getting cold. He reached up to the cord that turned on the heater above the bath and pulled it. There was a slight wrenching sound and the heater, with all bars fully lit, fell straight into the water. There was a frenzied hiss, sparks, and DeVere shot bolt upright in the bath with his hair on end. The heater fizzled out, and so did Mr. DeVere.

When he did not appear for breakfast in the SCR, the primus asked Mr. Pettibone and the Major whether they knew where DeVere might be. The steward when summoned had also not seen or heard anything of DeVere, but added:

"Strangest thing, Sir. Brian Gandivance's gone. Just gone. Left his things and all and left. No note. Told no one."

"Damn," said the primus. "He was such a good electrician. Go and get Mr. DeVere please. We're waiting for him."

A commotion in front quad drew them to the SCR windows. The Major opened them and asked a passing undergraduate what was up.

"Dunno, Sir."

The steward came bounding up the stairs, short of breath, hair flying and feet tripping over themselves.

"It's Mr. DeVere, Sir."

"Yes, man. What?"

"He's had an accident. He's dead."

"What?" said the primus. "He can't be. Call the doctor, and the nurse, get help."

"Allow me, Sir," said Mr. Pettibone. "I'll go over and take a gander (and he laughed inwardly at his wit). A short while later he returned.

"Yes, he's dead alright. Stone cold. The heater fell into the bath. Poor bastard," he said without any real sorrow behind his words.

"What a loss," said the primus. Turning to the Major he asked, "Do you know whether he had made a will in our favour?"

"No," said the Major. "He was going to, but only if we agreed to give him what he wanted first. That's what he told me. Did he tell you anything else, Pettibone?"

"No, Major, he didn't."

"Damn," said the primus.

Mr. Pettibone taking up his hat and coat bade goodbye to the primus and the Major. At the door he turned and looked at the two of them:

"*Benedictus, benedicat,*" he said, and walked out of the room.

Chapter 2: Oculi Omnium (The Eyes of All)

The tablet was situated as high up in the chapel and as inconspicuously as possible while still displaying a modicum of the respect due to the donor in whose memory it had been placed. It said in simple terms:

In memoriam St. John DeVere Benefactor.

There was no date, no engraving. Tom DeVere looked at his friend, Roderick James, son of Sir Julian James the surgeon, and asked him for his thoughts on the inscription.

"Rather plain."

"That's what I wondered," said Tom. "But the primus was insistent that Dad wouldn't have wanted it any other way. I did not agree with him, but the college was adamant. And Dad really wanted to be remembered and to be part of the fabric."

The tragic accident that had killed his father while he was taking his bath in the Queen's Room of St. Margaret's College, Oxford, had left Tom an orphan, albeit a rather rich one. Once the estate had been settled, he had made a substantial donation to the college in his father's name, as he knew his father would have wished. There were decided differences between father and son. Tom was sensitive and studious, inclined to be shy. His father had been worldly, perhaps a little too worldly, but had doted on his son. And Tom had loved his father deeply, despite their differing outlooks.

"You're going to be a gent, a real gent. Not like your dad. And remember, whatever you might be told, everything I did, I did for you. After your mother died, there was nothing and no one except you. You will have everything that you could want, I'll see to that, and those stuffy arses at the college will treat you like a king, after I've given them the cash they want."

"But, Dad," said Tom, "it doesn't work that way."

"Of course it does. You're too inexperienced in the ways of the world, boy. You didn't grow up selling crap from a barrow in Bermondsey like me. But you don't have to."

Tom shook his head. He knew that his way of the world and his father's were at polar opposites. Such attempts to bribe the governing body would likely build resentment and this would be taken out on him. Of course, in an ever-so-polite and indirect way but it would be there. Just as it had been at Dorchester. At least at first.

"Nuffink but the best school in the land for you," said St. John DeVere as he admired his son, splendid in the elegant but very distinctive school uniform. "I'll see that they treat you right, don't you worry."

Lavish gifts were made to the school: a library building and a gym annex; several funded scholarships for poor boys so that they could attend for free, provided they had the intellectual promise. And each of Tom's friends was subjected to an array of treats: holidays in Venice, boating parties on the Thames, shooting parties in Scotland and, for those inclined, seats at Lord's or the Oval.

Initially, this had the effect of isolating Tom from his peers, as also had the appearance of his father in his chauffeur-driven, bright red, coach-built Rolls Royce Silver Wraith limousine.

"Flash-Harry," said the boys. "Spiv." "Likely made his money in the black market." "I think he's a gangster," said another.

"No," said Tom, "he's a bookie." And it was that candour together with his open and kind personality that overcame the prejudice. He left Dorchester, head of his house and a member of a very posh self-selected club of boys entitled to enhance their dark uniforms with colourful ornamentation.

In his final year at school, he noticed that his reading had slowed, but he paid very little attention. There was so much more that he needed to do. He won a very competitive scholarship to St.

148

Margaret's College, a Birdstone (or "Berson," as the college slang called it). But he still needed to pass his school certificate examinations with decent marks to receive it. Academically, there was no problem. The problem was that it was taking a great deal longer for him to study than it had in the past. He sat at his books in his study and rubbed his eyes. Also, his favorite sport, cricket was letting him down. He had missed several easy catches.

'I think you need glasses,' he said to himself. 'Time enough for that in the vac.' And he went on with his studies.

He was up to read Greats (Classical Latin and Greek), and whereas his Latin was excellent, his Greek needed more effort. The Senior Classics master, Dr. Baker, had said as much and gave him extra lessons. But in his final year at Duster, as the school was affectionately known, his father had that terrible accident, and suddenly Tom's mind was diverted. Apart from the severe loss, the loss of a rough-but-kind father, he had to deal with the estate and all that that entailed. His father had been thoughtful in his choice of executors, and the lawyers and accountants had been kind and very helpful. As a minor, he required guardianship. His father had been in a quandary. None of his friends or associates would be up to the mark, he thought, as none were trustworthy, not even those who were out of prison. So it was with some surprise that Tom was notified by his attorney that a Major Sir John Cylburn, bursar of St. Margaret's College, had been appointed to this role under the terms of the will. Tom had not only never met this person but had never even heard of him. (He paid no attention whatever to the college prospectus or other bumpf in which the Major's name was listed.) The lawyer, who was an old friend of the family and had earned the elder DeVere's respect by his diligence in keeping him out of prison on more than one occasion — despite the weight of evidence against him — had explained:

"Tom, your father wanted someone who was going to be a guide and who could be close at hand to keep an eye on you. Shortly before his death he met Sir John, or the Major as he is known, and instantly made up his mind. Whatever else your father may have been (and the lawyer sniffed a little at this point) he was an excellent judge of character. He had to be in his line of business."

"Which was?" asked Tom. He knew that his father owned a very successful chain of betting shops, but wondered whether there was anything else he should be told.

"You know all about it, Tom. Your father was a very successful businessman. Shrewd and ..."

"And not particularly honest?" asked Tom.

The lawyer was taken aback by this insightful and accurate question from someone he considered very young and not a little naive. He decided to move on.

"You will be very well off once the estate is cleared through probate, and the staff will stay on so you should have no trouble keeping up the house and everything. And you might want a motor car, a nice sporty one perhaps."

Tom was not particularly interested in such matters. He was more concerned with Livy, Catullus, Lucretius and even that dry old stick Cicero whose *Oratio Pro Murena* was currently giving him nightmares. He wanted to be a classicist. "And we all know that classicists have class," so his father had said showing a rare instance of a sense of humour.

"And we have already received several good offers for your father's chain of betting shops, should you wish to sell." The lawyer continued. "Of course, you are now the majority shareholder but given that you are a minor it will be dependent on you and your guardian, with ... er ... advice from persons such as myself."

Tom gave the lawyer a shrewd glance and wondered how helpful and disinterested his advice would be.

After the benefaction was made to the college at Tom's insistence — although there had been nothing stipulated in his father's will — the tablet was ordered. The choice of words was suggested by the primus, the head of the college. Tom, whose mind at the time was on other things, eventually agreed with it.

And so now he was in his first term looking at the newly unveiled plaque. He had not been able to attend the small ceremony at its installation, as he had taken a short holiday and was out of the country. It was likely that the college knew this and chose the date accordingly.

Tom turned to his friend Roderick and asked him what it looked like.

"Can't you see for yourself?" asked Roderick.

"No. It's too high up for me."

"Oh, well it's, well it's … dignified."

"You mean plain?" asked Tom.

Roderick did not reply.

As they walked out of the chapel into the sunlight, Roderick James said:

"You know, Tom, and this is none of my business, but I was wondering whether you're alright. You seem a little strange, different from how you were at Duster," (the slang for Dorchester where they had been at school together, although not really close friends then).

"I'm okay. Why?"

"Well, for one thing, you seem clumsier. Walking into things and so on. And you ask for the oddest things."

"Like what?"

"Like in Hall asking for the salt when it's right in front of you on the table," Roderick replied.

"I'm distracted. I have a lot on my mind," said Tom, knowing that this was not the truth.

"Look, Tom. My dad's a doctor and he has a lot of good colleagues. Why don't you see him and get his opinion? Perhaps there's something wrong, really wrong. Or perhaps it's nothing at all."

"It's nothing at all," said Tom. "I've told you I've a lot on my mind."

"Like Claire?"

"No," said Tom, somewhat embarrassed that his girlfriend at Somerville should be thrown into the conversation.

"Well, I know that Claire's concerned, too. She told me about it a few days ago."

"Oh."

"Well at least think about seeing my father and getting an answer one way or another."

****

151

In Harley Street, Tom shook hands with Sir Julian James KCVO, MCh, FRCS, surgeon in ordinary to the royal household and sat down in a chair in his elegant consulting rooms.

"Roddy told me about you," said Sir Julian. "Of course, I am a general surgeon and not an ophthalmologist at that. But I did do some ophthalmology during my training, and we could just go through a few things, and if necessary, I could refer you on."

And they went through a few things. And he was referred on. Urgently to a Professor McCloud, a retina specialist at Moorfields Eye Hospital in London who kindly saw him the same day.

The news was not good. The condition was progressive, rapidly so, and there was no cure. Within a few months, a year at the outside, Tom would be completely blind. He would be considered partially sighted now, as it was. A prescription was given for glasses, and Tom was told that they might help in the short term. But only in the short term.

Tom's response was disbelief initially, and then with characteristic good humor he shrugged his shoulders and told Professor McCloud, "Well, I think I'd better start to learn Braille then, hadn't I?"

And they both laughed. "That's the spirit," said McCloud. "It's not the end of the world."

"Isn't it though?" replied Tom. His mood had suddenly changed.

On the train back to Oxford, Tom pondered over his next steps. Now that the news was sinking in, he was a little stunned and he needed advice. He decided that he would see the Major after Hall that evening. He had introduced himself to the Major and his wife in the long vac before he came up, and he saw that his father had made a very good choice of a guardian. They met several times after that, and subsequently he had been invited to dinner on many occasions once he had established himself in his rooms in college.

Lady Mary opened the door to the insistent knocking.

"So sorry, Lady Mary," replied Tom. "Is the Major in?"

"No, I'm afraid that he's still in college. Some matter that the primus and senior tutor want to discuss with him. No doubt something to do with the drains. It's always the drains these days. But come in, do, and you can wait for him here."

And she looked at him keenly.

152

"Tom, there's something the matter isn't there? Do you need to talk about it?"

"Yes, I'm afraid I do."

"Can I help? At least before John comes back, that is. You might need to talk to him, but perhaps I could be of use in the meantime? But first, take your coat off, and I'll make some tea. Or do you want something stronger?"

"No, tea will be good, thanks awfully." And Tom took his coat off, but misjudging the location of the coat hook, the coat fell to the floor. Lady Mary picked it up and hung it for him.

"Odd," she thought and went into the kitchen. She returned shortly afterwards with a tray of tea things and some biscuits. Tom was still in the hall.

"It's rather dark in here," he said.

"I suppose it is," she replied. "We'll go into the living room," and she led the way into the unlit room. Tom still stood in the hall, until she had switched on the light. Then he was able to enter. Although he had been to the house before, he was never entirely sure of its layout, and his eyes had become worse since his last visit.

He explained in a semi-cheerful way his visit to Roderick's father.

"Tom, that's awful," said Lady Mary. "What are you going to do?"

"Learn Braille I think." But this time there was no laughter. There was a catch in his voice, and although he turned away, Lady Mary could see that tears were streaming down his face.

"I am so sorry," she said, and getting up she put her arm around the boy's shoulder. He was now convulsed in sobs.

"I don't think I can explain this well," said Tom after he had collected himself a while later. "But I owe it to Dad to do well here and then afterwards. I can't if I'm blind."

"Of course, you can," said Lady Mary. "You still can get around the college and town."

"Yes, but I now need to ask for help. And it's embarrassing. I've had to give up cricket. And I can't finish my essays on time. My tutor is beginning to think I'm shirking … or drinking too much."

"You haven't told him?"

"No."

"Why on earth not?"

"Well, I only knew there was something really wrong today. I thought it was stress."

"But we'll tell him and the primus. The college will accommodate you. I'm sure they will."

"A blind classicist? Do you know how much reading is necessary? And as for Greek, well the less said the better"

"They can provide an aide. Or you can. You're very rich I believe. You can have all the help you need."

"That isn't the point. Anything I do has to be done by me. By me alone. With help, it will be all the others and I will get the credit. It's not the same thing. I need to show that I can stand on my own two feet. I owe that to myself and to Dad."

"You loved your father very much, didn't you?"

"Yes."

Lady Mary didn't want to tell Tom what she knew and the press had not yet discovered, about his father. She held her breath and then said, "You know, Tom, from what I've heard, your father was a very positive and pragmatic man. And also he cared about you deeply. He would take this as a setback, but he would think about it and definitely find a solution." She hoped that was so, but she wasn't so sure in her heart.

"I suppose so," said Tom and he looked at Mary with an anguished expression.

"I know this must be terrible, coming on top of the recent loss of your father. And then all of the legal matters that I know you are in the middle of, and also trying to settle in to a new environment. But you are in a very fortunate position. You have us; we will do anything to help, John and I. Also, you have your friends, especially Roderick who seems very fond of you."

"Yes, I know. But there's my whole life ahead. How am I going to cope? What will I do?"

"Don't you think there's an element of self-pity there? You will get over it. You're a fighter. I can see that. And you will always have help. Staff. And John and I will be there for you whatever and whenever you need it."

"Even after Oxford?"

"Even after Oxford!" Lady Mary carefully placed the cup to Tom's right together with a plate of biscuits and directed his attention to them.

"Lady Mary, thanks, but I can see them. If you don't mind, I really should be going anyway. It's late and I have an essay due tomorrow."

"Don't you want to wait for John?"

"No. I don't think so. You have been very kind. Thank you." And Lady Mary solicitously took him to the door and opened it.

"I don't think I'm ready for a white stick yet," said Tom.

Neither of them laughed.

****

The days rolled on. Tom was gradually getting used to the idea of his waning sight. He informed the primus and his tutor and they were duly sympathetic. They determined that he didn't need much extra help, but that a consultation with Moorfields in the near future might determine what aids would be useful and when. Tom was advised to make inquiries of his fellow classicists and friends in a general way to put together a plan regarding help with the logistics of his studies. Getting to and from lectures, having a friend read out a passage to him while Tom translated it and so on. His friends were most enthusiastic and assured him that they would help in any way and whenever he needed it.

Despite all of this, there were periods of deep despair. He knew that in a short while he wouldn't be able to see the beauty of the college, the beauty of the gardens, the beauty of the world. He was overcome by a sense of helplessness. And what about Claire? Would she always be at his side? He had grown increasingly fond of her, and she of him. He had determined to tell her of his problems, and she responded by telling him that she didn't think she would be able to cope. She was too young to be tied to an invalid. And she had her own career to think of. Naturally, she didn't put it like that. It was more drawn out and less to the point, but Tom understood. And slowly they drifted apart.

He was heartbroken. And that added to his growing sense of despair. He suddenly knew that he wouldn't have the stamina to continue with his course of study. It was getting too hard already. It would be harder. And despite all of the help that was offered, his gloom overspread any sense of reason. But still he persevered and struggled. And there were good days. Days when he felt the sunshine and knew that at least would always be with him. And also music. Music was important to him. And he wasn't deaf and not likely to become deaf either. So, there were compensations.

One night, a dark one, no moonlight, Tom was being assisted back to his set by Roderick.

"Good night, Tom. Do you need me to help you with anything, or will you be okay?"

"Thanks, Roddy, I think that I can still undress on my own."

Roderick blushed and walked off humming a tune softly to himself. Tom stopped to listen as the sound faded away in the distance. Reaching in his pocket for the key, he thought about how truly fortunate he was in his friends. He turned the key in the lock and as he walked into the room, the room illuminated.

"Don't be frightened," said a voice, a voice that Tom did not recognize. He turned towards it and saw the vague outline of a figure in the shadows behind the lamp that the man had just switched on. He stepped forward, and Tom saw a young man, probably only one or two years older than he, with unkempt hair and an unshaven face. His clothes were dirty and his shoes had clearly seen better days. And the man had a gun. It was pointed at him. That much he could see. Tom was startled and in trying to back out of the room, he tripped over a chair behind him and fell to the ground. The young man stepped forward and looked down.

"You're Tom, aren't you? Tom DeVere? My father knew yours. I'm Brian Gandivance." Tom looked at him questioningly.

"You haven't a clue, have you? Not a clue at all. Well, I'm going to change that." And he bent down and gently gave Tom a hand up. Seeing that Tom was looking around him and clearly had some difficulty, he asked, "You okay?"

"No, I'm blind." Why he came out with this overstatement he had no idea. Perhaps it was the shock of this intruder in his room. Perhaps he thought to engage this man's sympathy.

156

Gandivance gave a low whistle. "Well, you're a poor bastard, aren't you just?" And the tone was not sympathetic. "I don't suppose you'll be able to make me a cup of tea, you poor sod."

"The tea's over there. I can make it. I can see a bit. And there's whisky if you want." Tom was very frightened. He neither liked the tone nor the appearance of Mr. Gandivance. Both were menacing and distinctly so.

"I'll have some whisky," said Gandivance, and walked over to the table and poured himself a large tumbler full. He did not offer Tom anything.

"What do you want?" asked Tom in a high-pitched voice.

"I'll come to that after I've had a drink," he said as he sat down and eyed Tom slowly.

"I've come to tell you about your father."

"What could you possibly know about him?"

"Your father and my father were associates. Close associates. Of course, he wasn't Mr. Snooty DeVere then. Only Reggie Gall of Bermondsey." Tom did not say anything. "That was probably when you were very small and just a wee little piece of shit. Back then the two of them, and some others that they knew, had the idea to pull off a robbery. A big one. Your father was the mastermind of that, he was."

"I ... I don't believe you."

"Of course you don't. I didn't expect you to. But anyway, believe it or not, your dad and mine and these three other chaps pulled off the robbery. Your father, however, wanted the loot for himself. He hired a clever lawyer and gave evidence against all of them. All of them except my dad. He needed his help and they provided each other with an alibi."

"And you know this because ...?"

"Because, my dad told me. Or told me so in a letter."

"Why didn't your father tell you this himself?"

"I'm coming to that." Tom got up from the chair he was sitting in.

"I don't have to listen to this. Get out!"

"No, I'm not leaving. You have to hear it. It'll be good for your soul."

157

"Well, if you won't go, I will," and Tom turned 'round and took a step towards the door.

"If you go now, you'll never find out." As Tom opened the door, he said, "I killed your father."

Bewildered, Tom turned around.

"Close the door," said Gandivance, and then continued. "Before you came here, I was the college electrician, or at least an assistant electrician. I heard DeVere and another bloke talking in Hall. I figured out who DeVere really was. Reggie Gall, who killed my dad. I rigged up the heater so that when he pulled the cord it would come off the wall and fall into the bath. I couldn't be sure that he would have a bath, or even when. But I took a chance. And if that didn't work, well there would be other ways. Other occasions. I was sure of that."

"But why?" asked Tom.

"Because your dad killed mine. After the talk died down and the pair of them went free, your dad wanted everything for himself. So he lured my father somewhere, killed him, and got rid of the body. It was never found. He disappeared. No one cared. Except my mother. And me. The poor old bugger was a good dad to me. That was a long time ago. But before he died, he wrote a letter, and in it he gave everything away and explained about your dad. He said if anything happened to him, then we should go to the police and give them the letter."

"And I suppose with the usual postal delay it only took 10 years to get to them," said Tom.

"Sarky, aren't we? No, it took longer than that. My mum lost the letter. She simply put it somewhere and then forgot about it. She never had all her forks in the drawer, my mum. Spent the last few years in the looney bin. Schizophrenia they said. She died last year, and in going through her things, I found the letter. It was in a box that she never opened. Said that it contained the secrets of the universe and a spirit that was watching over her and telling her what to do. She said that if we opened it then she would die. I knew that was all bullshit, but I didn't know about the letter then. But I do now. Want to see it?"

And he thrust it into Tom's face. "Of course, you poor bastard, you probably can't read, can you." And before Tom could answer he said, "I'll read it to you." He did so, and gradually Tom understood or he thought he did. He still wasn't completely sure. He didn't want to be.

"I'm going now. But I'll be back. I wouldn't tell the police or the college about our chat. If you do, then I'll have to show them the letter."

"They won't believe you."

"Oh, they'll believe it alright. It wouldn't be too difficult to check. Your father was quite clever I suppose about the accidental drowning and no body being discovered, then the surgery to his face and a new identity. Quite easy these days what with the war, the disruption, and the loss of records in bombing. But dig deep enough …" And he opened the door and vanished into the night.

Tom sat and stared at the wall for a while. Then he got up and slowly made his way to the door of his bedroom. He wasn't sure what to do. As he walked, he tripped over an object, a heavy object that had fallen onto the floor. He picked it up. It was round in part, in part flat, cold to the touch and somehow fitted his hand perfectly.

Absentmindedly, he walked into the bedroom and sat on the bed. Feeling the thing, 'that man must have dropped it,' he thought. Or perhaps he left it there. On purpose. And then the feeling of blank despair came over him. These were getting more frequent now. There was the prospect of his complete blindness, the loss of his future, the loss of Claire, his father's death, and now this. Even if this couldn't be proved, it would raise enough questions. He thought and thought. Speak to the Major and Lady Mary in the morning. He knew that they would be understanding and give him good advice. But did he want to go on any more? Of course he did. His father would want him to. So would his friends. In a funny way, so would Claire. All of them would help. His father would be proud of him. Very proud. And it would all be a lie.

The sound of the shot reverberated from the room out over Front Quad; a startled bird, alarmed, flew up into the sky.

Chapter 3: Tu Das Escam (You give us meat)

Mr. Pettibone was enjoying his Saturday morning. Though it was raining outside, he had sunshine in his heart. The toast was crisp, the tea of the exact strength that he liked, and there was nothing too disconcerting in the morning paper. Additionally, he was contemplating where he would go later in the day for a brief overnighter. For Mr. Pettibone had bought a car. Not a new one, but a secondhand Morris, pre-war, and in good working order. And of respectable reliability. Or so he had been advised by Mr. Settle, the secondhand car dealer. It had been the Major who had put him up to the idea.

"What you need, Pettibone, is a car," he had said when he last came to London and they had enjoyed lunch together.

"What on earth for?" Mr. Pettibone had replied, somewhat taken aback.

"Two reasons: One that you need it for your business. You have to make trips to the country from time to time to value the contents of houses that many unfortunate people are nowadays forced to sell. And relying on trains and buses can be expensive and not always reliable."

"Too true," said Mr. Pettibone and nodded.

"Then there is the sheer enjoyment. The sense of freedom. If you want to go for a ride, you can. You can go anywhere. Whenever you want."

"But there's petrol rationing."

"True. There is a cost."

"Yes, and cars aren't cheap either."

"But you must offset that against the sheer pleasure and convenience. And it could help your business by being able to visit potential clients in more out-of-the-way places."

Mr. Pettibone, of Pettibone, Sons and Langford, Dealers and Valuers of Fine Antiques, pondered this for a while.

"If you want, Pettibone, I can give you a few lessons and you can see how you like it." And he did, and Pettibone did. And so, that is how Mr. Pettibone bought his first car. There had been more driving lessons and then the dreaded test. London examiners were notoriously keen on failing people to keep drivers off the road. But he was lucky, and the examiner passed him the first time.

He got up from his breakfast table and took out a brand-new Shell map of Staybrookshire (abbreviated to Stanx). In the past, he had loathed the country, believing it vacant and uncivilized. A few jaunts with the Major had partially eclipsed this opinion, and he contemplated villages and Norman churches in a new light. His first visit to Stanx had not been a spectacular success, and in the end had cost him virtually all of his money, but he thought he could test his newfound passion for driving and interest in the countryside with a trip to this old haunt.

As he was poring over the map, after having poured his third cup of tea, there was a sharp rap on the door. Reluctantly, Mr. Pettibone put the map down and moved towards the door of the flat. But before he could open it there came a longer series of raps.

"Alright, alright, I'm coming," he said. "Keep your hair on."

And with that, he loosened the chain and opened the Mortis lock. Two men were outside. A taller and a shorter one, in an ordinary Macintosh raincoat and the other in a plain suit. Their hair was slicked down with oil, and they exuded a no-nonsense officialdom that Mr. Pettibone immediately recognized.

"Mr. Pettibone?"

"Yes," he said, somewhat alarmed.

"Mr. Albert Pettibone?"

"The same," said Mr. Pettibone.

"May we come in?"

"Of course," Mr. Pettibone said and waived the policemen politely into the hall and then ushered them into the sitting room. Mr.

161

Pettibone was on his guard. In his line of business and with his past, he had to be.

"Won't you gentlemen, sit down? Can I get you anything? Tea or something else?"

"No, thank you, Sir," said the taller of the two, taking out his notebook. There was a silence as the two policemen were clearly looking around the room for anything out of the ordinary: stolen items, a corpse, and other such common items as every well-ordered household might have on open display.

Showing their warrant cards, the short and stout man with greying blond hair introduced them.

"I'm Inspector Blake of the CID, and this is Detective Sergeant Balls."

"Pleased to meet you," said Mr. Pettibone, and tried to soften the note of anxiety that he was sure had crept into his voice. "Always happy to help the police, I am," he lied.

I'm sure you're a busy man, Mr. Pettibone, so we shan't detain you long. By the way, what is your line of business?"

"I'm an antiques dealer and estate valuer," said Mr. Pettibone.

The two policemen exchanged glances. They had experienced frequent dealings with persons of that sort.

"Do you, er, did you, know a Mr. Settle? Stanley Settle of Brixton."

"Well, I don't know him. I bought a car from him."

"Recently?"
"Yes."
"When?"
"About three weeks ago."

And his mind wandered back to the purchase of the car. It had happened like this: A friend of his just out of the Scrubs was looking for a job, and Mr. Pettibone — ever eager to do a good turn — had bought him tea in a Hammersmith Cafe, just down the road from the prison. He had given this man a number to call and said that he would put in a good word with the proprietor of the printers who were looking for help. He also lent the man a fiver and said, "That should be good for a few weeks until you can get a job. Should be able to at least find a roof over your head. And here is my number. Call me if you need anything."

"Bless you, Bert," said the man. "This here thing was a mistake. It's always us who suffer. Not them rich folks. They're all against us. The system is against us. It was all a mistake, a misunderstanding. I shouldn't have been found guilty. They got the wrong man. It was a big mistake."

"Well, 10 years without parole is a long time to serve for a mistake. Pity that the nightwatchman had such a soft skull."

"It's a mistake, like I said. I was just having a kip inside the factory and this bloke came along. I called out to him, and he just seemed to fall and hit his head."

"Fell against your hammer. Funny how you happened to have that with you. And the jemmy. I suppose you were out for a night at the Palladium and just happened to go into the factory for a quick nap before the evening's entertainment? Together with the tools, in case your limousine broke down."

"Don't be like that, Bert," said the man.

Changing the subject, Mr. Pettibone said, "Talking of limousines, I'm going to buy a car."

"Well, perhaps I can help you. In return like. I've a friend, Stan Settle; he runs a car business down Brixton way."

Mr. Pettibone looked hard at the man. "Look, I need to buy a regular car. Not one wot's been pinched. Has to be on the up and up. My line of business …"

"Bert, you can't fool me. If you could buy something on the cheap no questions asked, you would. Just to save you a few hundred quid."

"Nah. Not now. I'm respectable. Completely straight and all my dealings have to be, too. Any friend of yours, well I would have to be sure that they weren't handy with a hammer for starters."

"Nah, Stan is my brother-in-law. Never been in trouble with the law, he hasn't." And after a little more conversation, the man gave Mr. Pettibone the telephone number of the brother-in-law and two days later he was face to face with Mr. Stanley Settle.

"This car is exactly what you need, Mr. Pettibone," said Stan. "It's economical and reliable. Bought it off a vicar I did. 1938 Morris, good condition, very low mileage."

"Before or after you put the clock back?" asked Mr. Pettibone.

"I'm hurt, deeply hurt, Mr. Pettibone. I run a respectable business. All above board."

Mr. Pettibone was duly skeptical. He had never heard of an honest second-hand car dealer before. But he chose to ignore his suspicions as this was a really good deal. And if there was anything that Mr. Pettibone liked it was a good deal. After everything was settled in the cold, drafty hut that served as an office, Stan took Mr. Pettibone to the local pub for a drink. Warming up over a pint of Bass or three, they got to talk and found that they had many things in common. One of which was always trying to be helpful to their fellow man. Supplying whatever was needed in these difficult post-war times. Rationing had made the staples of everyday life difficult to obtain and very expensive. Food being key amongst them.

"Wasn't always a car dealer, Bert," said Stan.

"No?"

"Nah. I used to be a butcher. Now there's a tough job. Takes years of training. Difficult. Had me own butcher's shop. Then came the war and had to close down. After the war, well it was difficult to start up again, and an old army chum put me in this line of business. Cars. But I always have kept me hand in. Run a small butcher's as a side line. Meat supply. Wholesale. Not to individuals, but to businesses. Restaurants and things like that. In a small way. But I'd like to get back in. Grow the business. Me heart's not really in cars. Not really. Want to get back into meat. Perhaps you know of someone who might need some meat, cheap, good cuts. And also there's processed food that I do. Hamburger meat, all that grinded stuff."

"Thanks," said Mr. Pettibone. "I'll remember that." And he forgot completely until a few days later when he had a call from the Major.

"Pettibone, I wonder whether you can help us?"

Mr. Pettibone was always eager to help the Major, except with anything that might impinge on his own self-respect. Mr. Pettibone was protective of his dignity. He owed that to himself, and he owed a lot to the Major. Occasionally, the two concerns clashed.

"Always happy to help, Major, you know that."

The Oxford college where the Major was the bursar needed some food. Feeding a hundred and fifty young men, many of them

164

recently out of the army, was an expensive and difficult business. And the Major was doing his best. But there had been a period when his suppliers could not deliver in adequate quantity.

"It's the war," they said.

"But the war's over. Has been for a few years. You mean that someone's given you a better price."

And they negotiated, but the Major did not have the budget. And so after talking things over with his wife, Lady Mary, he followed up on her recommendation.

"Why don't you ask that little friend of yours? He has contacts," she had said.

"You don't like him, Mary, do you?"

"Not really, no. I don't know what it is, but I just cannot warm to him. And given what he did to you in the past, I don't have a clue what it is that you see in him. But he has proved useful to you, and if you trust him, why not give him a call."

"So Pettibone, can you help?" asked the Major after explaining what he needed.

"Funny you should ask, Major, but I think I can." And after the conversation ended, Mr. Pettibone set about rummaging in his pockets for Stanley Settle's telephone number.

"Hello, Bert," said Stan. "How's tricks?" There was a faint note of anxiety in his voice.

"No, everything's okay with the car," said Mr. Pettibone acknowledging to himself what the cause of Stan's muted anxiety might be. "I want to put you into a line of business. And it might prove a good contact for you."

"I'm all ears."

"A friend of mine runs the kitchens for a posh Oxford college. He needs meat. A lot of it. Good quality …"

"And cheap?"

"And cheap."

"Well, you've come to the right man. How much and what does he want?"

165

"Dunno. But I'll give him your number and you two can settle the details." And with that, Mr. Pettibone hung up.

A week later, the Major rang Mr. Pettibone. "You know that friend of yours?"

"Yes."

"Well, I've been trying to reach him. And I can't get through. No one answers. Do I have the right number?"

And they checked. And it was the right number.

"Sorry, Major. Tell you what I'll do. I'll give him a ring myself. And if there's no reply, I'll go down to his car lot and see if I can find him there.

"Well, it's getting rather urgent, Pettibone. We're desperately short. Don't want to have to feed the lads with the college cat."

So after several unsuccessful attempts to reach Stan Settle on the phone, Mr. Pettibone got into his car and drove down to Brixton. The lot was there and still full of cars. But the hut where he had transacted his business was locked and empty. Mr. Pettibone, with his hands in his pockets, walked around the lot. There was no sign of life, no sign of hide or hair. That was a week ago.

Sergeant Balls coughed, and Mr. Pettibone was brought back from his reverie.

"So, you have had dealings with him?"

"In a way, yes."

"Did you know about his meat business?"

"Yes, I did. I recommended him to a friend of mine."

"You did now, did you?" The two policemen's interest was clearly aroused.

"Is that important?"

"Very," said the inspector. "What line of business was your friend in?"

"He's the bursar of St. Margaret's College, Oxford," said Mr. Pettibone.

"Oh!" Sergeant Balls was clearly surprised.

"Not what you were expecting, eh?" said Mr. Pettibone.

"Do you know anything about Settle?"

"Nothing other than what I told you. And also that I had tried to put the bursar in contact with him, without success. And I have also been down to try to find him."

"When was that?"

"Tuesday, last."

"Did you find him?"

"No. Didn't see hide nor hair of him."

"Very appropriate choice of words in the circumstances," said the inspector. "We have found him."

"Oh, good. Is he alright?"

"Not really. He went all to pieces. We found parts of him at his butcher's shop. He had been put through the machine that chops up meat."

"What? How do you know it's him?"

"We have his fingerprints on file. They matched a finger."

"A finger?"

"Yes, we only found one."

"And there was another thing we found. A wallet. Belonging to a Mr. Gandivance. Know him?"

"No. But I have heard the name somewhere."

"Well, he disappeared some years ago. Without a trace. Was involved in a big bank robbery with a Reggie Gall. We haven't found him either. Heard of him, have you?"

"No, don't think I have." Mr. Pettibone hoped that the policemen wouldn't detect the lie.

"So, what's it all about and why are you questioning me?"

"You were the last entry in his diary. I think that you have explained your connection, but I have to warn you that we will have to go into all of that further. But I don't mind telling you that Mr. Stanley Settle had many friends, many odd friends at that. His most recent ones were the Groote brothers."

"Not those East End thugs?"

"The very same. Mr. Settle's business proved to be very useful to them and very lucrative to him. He helped them get rid of annoying little matters."

167

"Like bodies?"

"Like bodies. And without a corpus delicti, there couldn't be any case against them. At least that is what they thought. But with Gandivance's wallet and some other things we found at Settle's shop, we might have a case. By the way, I wouldn't go telling them about our little chat if I were you. It might be bad for your health."

"Me?" said Mr. Pettibone in surprise. "I don't know them. Wouldn't know them from Adam."

"Well, that's alright then." And the two detectives got up and took their leave.

"Well, I'm damned," exclaimed Mr. Pettibone as he picked up the telephone in his trembling hands to call the Major.

And in frightened tones, Mr. Pettibone retailed the meeting that he had just had.

"Extraordinary. Well, the young blighters here had a narrow escape. A case of not *tu das escam*."

"What, Major? What's that?" said Mr. Pettibone.

"*Tu das escam.* You give us meat. It's part of the college grace."

"I see," said Mr. Pettibone as he put the receiver down gently into its holder.

Chapter 4: Tempore Illo Opportuno
(At the appropriate time)

———————⋅⟨∞⟩⋅———————

The college chapel was looking unaccustomedly festive. The gloom was dissipated by the lit candles and the sunlight flooding through the mediaeval stained glass. The governing body added a touch of colour being in full academic dress, the crimson hoods of the masters and the scarlet of the doctors' robes providing a lively touch. How ironic, thought Mr. Pettibone, given that this was a memorial service, a service in memory of Tom DeVere (son of St. John DeVere) who had perished in the tragic accident in the Queen's Room of the college). Tom had taken his own life 'while the balance of his mind was in doubt' (according to the inquest) and the college trying to recover from the embarrassment of losing an undergraduate in these circumstances.

Mr. Pettibone had vaguely known St. John DeVere, formerly Reggie Gall of dubious antecedents and worse. He sat there next to the Major and Lady Mary with the thought that life, and even death, was so very strange … strange and unpredictable. Surrounded by the monuments and plaques memorializing dead Chasians and benefactors, he shrugged his shoulders and thought to himself, 'just get on with life and don't think too hard. It's over soon anyway, so why bother?'

The Major, on the other hand, was obviously disconsolate. He had lost a young man to whom he had been the guardian during his minority and had looked on him as a son. The Major had no children of his own, and this was the second loss of someone to whom he was *in loco parentis*. Lady Mary, his wife, held his hand and gently caressed it

169

while the Major tried to keep the tears from flowing. He had decided not to wear his uniform, as he doubted that he could keep a stiff upper lip during the service and consequently did not want to disgrace the Regiment.

Across the aisle, a cadre of undergraduates and some parents assembled in the pews. In the front row sat Tom's closest friends, Roddy James and that auburn-haired boy who looked about 12 and was constantly pushing a thick tuft off his forehead. Next to him was a tall, grey-haired, stern man whom Mr. Pettibone had not seen before, but in observing the mannerisms thought that this might be the boy's father. Whereas Roddy was wearing a scholar's long gown, the boy was wearing a bum-warmer, the short gown that commoners wore, which reached down to the buttocks and had streamers attached on either side. With these in mediaeval times, students could be stopped and fastened on by either town or university authorities if caught in some misdemeanor. The senior organ scholar was playing a Bach prelude, and although Mr. Pettibone did not care much for classical music, he was taken with the professionalism of the performance. The chapel was filled with the sonorous strains, which rose, fell, rose again, and cascaded down from the high vault of the chapel to delight the audience.

As the verger entered with ceremonial wand, the college stood. The choir followed each in crimson cassocks (the college colour), ruffs, and white surplice. They were followed by the chaplain and finally by the primus, Lord Hinchbury, a cousin of Lady Mary's. A hymn was sung, and then the service commenced. In due course, Lord Hinchbury approached the large, brass, seventeenth-century lectern and read an eulogy:

"The loss of a life in tragic circumstances is difficult to bear. Doubly so, is it when that life is taken in its prime. Many of us have seen so much of this terrible waste, the waste of the young taken in war when they had their whole span ahead of them; the loss of the contributions that they would have made. But now, they are just a passing thought in the minds of those who mourn them. It is our job to remember them, as we remember with regret the passing of Tom DeVere. Tom was one of our very

170

finest undergraduates, a Birdstone scholar with a bright future ahead of him. We would undoubtedly have been happy to welcome him to the fellowship of this college as a classicist of merit and distinction. In the words of our Grace: *Tempore illo opportuno*, there is an appropriate time for everything. It is hard to see what was appropriate about the tragic loss of this young life, so full of promise."

At this point, Mr. Pettibone's attention wandered; the auburn-haired boy and his father were engaged in some type of argument, but Mr. Pettibone could not hear what was passing between them in muffled tones. Seated next to the Major, he felt rather than heard the convulsive sobs that he was ineffectually trying to suppress. Lady Mary now gripped her husband's arm and, like so many of her kind, bearing the strain with fortitude and courage. Mr. Pettibone thought that she was a perfect match for the Major and was happy for him.

The service continued winding its mournful way with a delicate grace. At its end, after the choir, chaplain, primus, and governing body had shuffled out, the auburn-haired boy's father walked across the nave and approached the group. The boy trotted after his father and looked decidedly upset.

"Hello, Cylburn. Sorry about Tom. You were his guardian, I believe?"

"Yes."

The Major turned to Lady Mary and introduced the man.

"Mary, this is Colonel Sharp; he and I were in the army together during the war." The Major's tone was cold and the colonel was trying to smooth over the obvious tension between them with a broad smile, which to Mr. Pettibone, reeked of insincerity.

"It is so good of you to come," said the Major lamely, and he turned to the boy.

"It must be hard for you," he said.

"Yes, sir, it is. We were great friends." And the boy looked as if he were about to dissolve in tears.

"Oh, for heaven's sake, Simon," said his father. "Stop blubbering and pull yourself together."

And Mr. Pettibone thought how strange it was that the English treated their dogs like children and their children like dogs.

"Run along now," the colonel said. Inappropriate choice of words thought Mr. Pettibone. The boy, despite his pre-pubertal appearance, was clearly very bright and well-behaved. He felt his father should have shown more respect.

"Dad!" said the boy.

"Don't call me 'Dad.' I've told you that before." The boy was greatly embarrassed by this, flushed a bright crimson, and stomped off with head bowed.

"Well, Colonel, are you staying or going back to London?" asked the Major.

"I'm going straight back and won't stay for lunch. But actually, I've come over to have a word with Mr. Pettibone here."

"Me?" said Mr. Pettibone, taken aback. He had never met the colonel before and from what he had just seen was glad of that.

"Cylburn, this must be awful for you. I don't want to detain you and your wife any longer." And the Major and his wife walked down the nave slowly, hand in hand and out of the chapel.

"Now, Pettibone, come over here." Mr. Pettibone reluctantly did what he was commanded.

"You, of course, know the primus," the colonel added.

"Er, yes, er, but not well. He was a customer of mine a few years back. Pettibone, Sons and Langford, you know. Dealers and valuers of fine antiques. Perhaps you would like my card?"

"Not now, Pettibone, not now."

"As you wish. First class, absolutely first class," said Mr. Pettibone, who used that form of words in many different circumstances, in this case when he was nervous and wary.

"Well, that is why I'm here. I believe you handled several transactions on his behalf?"

"Yes, the icons."

"Indeed, the Russian icons. The primus seemed to have acquired a large collection. Valuable, very valuable indeed. Know how he got them, do you?"

"No, I don't. Generally, I like to know provenance, but Lord Hinchbury was very vague on that point. Lots of things happened during the war. Perhaps he got them from some bombed church or other."

"Quite. Just so, Pettibone, just so. In your line of business, I am sure that it doesn't pay to be too inquisitive."

Mr. Pettibone was not pleased with this imputation of dishonesty.

"Everything I do is above board," he said.

"And with your record," said the colonel, referring to Mr. Pettibone's sojourn at Her Majesty's pleasure, "you can't be too careful, I agree." The ironic tone was not lost on Mr. Pettibone.

"Pettibone, I want you to do me a favour, or rather my employers."

"What? Why?"

"The icons were of great interest to my superiors and, consequently, to me. We have traced them to a gentleman, a white Russian who said that he had brought them out after the revolution. Actually, our information shows a different origin; they were brought over in the diplomatic bag from Russia, by a courier at the Russian embassy."

"What's this got to do with Lord Hinchbury, or me for that matter?"

"I'm coming to that. Your Lord Hinchbury is rather an interesting creature. Before the war he had decided views, not uncommon at the time when there was little to oppose fascism. He had joined the communist party and was recruited by Moscow as an enterprising young man. Not that uncommon either. What was more to the point, though, was that he proved very active in finding other likely candidates for a similar role. The Russians were looking for young people who would in time occupy positions of power. They would be, in Stalin's words, useful idiots. Pawns who would do their bidding, especially when it came to intelligence."

"Wot?" said Mr. Pettibone, increasingly alarmed at the way things were going.

"Hinchbury was a most valuable asset. As a young Fellow of this college, he identified to his handlers certain likely candidates among the undergraduates. When he was in intelligence during the war, actually in my department as it happens, we became aware that he might be providing the Russians with information. As they were our

173

allies at the time, we were not too concerned and provided him with stuff that we wanted them to know."

"Did he know that?" asked Mr. Pettibone.

"No. We assessed that he was too committed to be turned. He maintained his links with British military intelligence for some time after the war. He still had access to secret information. Through friends. Not top secret. But still of some importance. But now, things are different and the view of my superiors is that Russia has become a subversive threat and Lord Hinchbury's activities are treasonous. He had suddenly been provided with a large collection of Russian icons, and that is where you come in."

"Oh," said Mr. Pettibone dejectedly.

"Yes. He used the icons to smuggle out microfilm. You were engaged to be the agent who ..."

"Now that you mention it, it was odd that not long after he came to my shop, a Czech emigre asked me to find some icons for him, which I did."

"Which you did. Just so. Hinchbury got his cash and the Russians got their information. Some of it, I have to say, was a little doctored by us, but some of it was pure, beyond our control and put lives at risk."

"So?"

"This had to stop. We had a meeting with him and told him that we knew all about what he had done and was continuing to do. In exchange for some information that he offered us, we were prepared to give him a certain degree of immunity. But when he became the head of this college, we were concerned. We now believe that he is actively trying to recruit again. From this college."

"Wot's this to do with me?" asked Mr. Pettibone.

"We want him to stop. I have been to see him, but he just laughed. In a roundabout sort of way, he seemed to want proof that we knew all about him. And that is where you come in. Tell him that MI6 has approached you and that you may have no alternative but to provide the evidence they need. You will also say that you have been told that the new government is less likely to support him than before. There could be questions in the House of Commons, and everything would come out. This can be stopped, I think, if he resigns from all public offices ..."

"You mean as primus?" said Mr. Pettibone.

"Precisely so. He is to go into obscurity, and I will do my best to persuade the Home Secretary that revealing everything would be an embarrassment to MI6 as well as to the government. What might the public think if they found out that a traitor had been protected by the powers that be? Especially that he was still able to smuggle out information to a hostile power while under our surveillance. Information that we did not know he had in his possession."

"I don't think I want to do your dirty work for you, Colonel Sharp."

"Oh, but Pettibone, you have no choice. None at all. We intercepted one of the icons. We had the Czech emigre under observation for some time. We found the microfilm, and for all we know, you were part of the whole scheme. A Russian agent, perhaps?"

"Don't be absurd," Mr. Pettibone was beginning to sweat.

"I'm not being absurd, but realistic. Things could become very tricky for you. I don't suppose you have had any dealings with MI6, have you?"

"No."

"No, and you don't want to, either. So if you don't want to end up in prison again, I suggest that you think very carefully and do exactly what I say. Oh, and there is another small thing."

The colonel took out a piece of paper from his breast pocket.

"Sign this," he said, and unscrewing the cap of his fountain pen, he handed both to Mr. Pettibone.

Mr. Pettibone faltered.

"Look, I have to get back to London for a meeting. I don't have all day. Sign it now."

"What is it?"

"Just a formality."

Mr. Pettibone knew when he was beaten and signed.

"In case you were thinking of going to the press or telling anyone of our little conversation here today, I must advise you that you have just signed the official secrets act and that any such move would be a contravention for which there are very severe penalties."

Mr. Pettibone looked down. The colonel marched off, the heels of his shoes making a clacking sound on the tessellated floor.

A few days later, Mr. Pettibone stood in the hallway of the Primus' lodgings.

"There's a funny-looking man outside to see you, David," said the primus' wife. "A Mr. Pettibone."

"Oh, him. Send him in, please."

"Well, Pettibone, come in. What can I do for you?" The primus' cheery tone changed when Mr. Pettibone told him the reason for his visit.

"Preposterous! I have to resign? And move to some cottage in the country far from civilization and my clubs? And my tailor?"

"The colonel was most insistent, Sir," said Mr. Pettibone. "And, I must tell you that I have been forced to confirm the icon issue and to explain all what I know. So they have all the links in the chain."

"But if I go, who could replace me here? I can't think of anyone suitable."

"No one is irreplaceable; I'm sure you could name one or two. I know I could."

Lord Hinchbury got up and walked towards the whisky decanter. With shaking hands, he poured himself a stiff drink. Turning to Mr. Pettibone:

"I'll think about it," he said.

****

As the moving van wobbled away from the primus' lodgings later that year, Mr. Pettibone, on a brief visit to the Major, gazed after it and then crossed the road. He walked through the gateway and into St. Margaret's. He stopped in front of the glass case in which college notices were displayed. In addition to the usual:

Gentlemen are reminded that letting off fire extinguishers in college is strictly forbidden except in the event of fire. Severe penalties will accrue, up to and including rustication.

There was another:

> The Visitor and Governing Body are pleased to announce the appointment of Sir John Cylburn Bt, DSO, MC, MA, sometime Scholar of Cardinal College, Oxford, and formerly bursar to the post of primus of St. Margaret's College.

Mr. Pettibone smiled a contented smile.

'*Tempore illo opportuno*,' he said to himself, and he walked out into the sunlight of front quad.

END

ACKNOWLEDGEMENTS

It is unlikely that any work proceeds in a vacuum. Consequently, I thank the following for providing the air that made this book, and Mr. Pettibone, possible. Their encouragement and willingness to read the chapters and to provide helpful feedback is much appreciated. They are (in no particular order): Mary Handley, Bill Handley, Laura Malkus, Andrew Cosner, Sylvia Eggleston-Wehr, Bettina Jenkins and Alexander Razumovsky. I should also like to thank my editor Mary Angela Davids for her unfailing help and expertise. For the mentorship, time and kindness of award-winning author Susan Reiss I am indeed indebted.

STEPHEN OPPENHEIMER

Stephen has been writing for as long as he can remember. Or at least, for as long as he remembers holding a pen. Short stories and satirical plays and even verse in the style of fellow Mertonian EC Bentley flowed easily at school and university, not always to universal delight. Multilingual, he can be misunderstood in German, and possibly even French and Italian. In recent years he has led a class in German literature.

After leaving Oxford, Stephen went to medical school in London and subsequently continued training in general medicine, cardiology and neurology in which he specialized. As a neuroscientist, his research identified centres of representation of the heart within the brain, and the concept that cardiac control can be lateralized with different functions separated according to location on the right or left side of the brain. Continuing his writing, this time in the scientific arena, Stephen has published several hundred peer-reviewed papers and reviews on this subject, with research funded by the National Institutes of Health and the American Heart Foundation among others.

To earn a living Stephen held faculty appointments in Neurology, Cardiology and Neurosurgery variously at Johns Hopkins University, Vanderbilt, and Pennsylvania State Universities.

A different form of creative writing presented itself when, following the death of his wife in 2020 the covid era struck. Unable to leave his flat and travel in the wider world, Stephen decided to bring the wider world into his flat. And so Mr. Pettibone paid a visit and with Stephen wrote the first in a series of mystery novels about people characterized by 'self-directed morality.' In interviews Stephen has said that he is fascinated not only by what people say, but what they leave unsaid. The influence of past experiences, and the scars these cleave and how they influence moral decision-making are a major theme of his work, and surface metaphorically in his writing.